Stoppage Time

Helen Shacklady

Published in 2003 by Onlywomen Press Ltd, London, UK.

With financial support from Arts Council England

ISBN 0-906500-78-8

British Library Cataloguing-in-Publication Data.
A Catalogue record for this book is available from the British Library.

Copyright © Helen Shacklady, 2003
Cover design © Spark Design, 2003

Typeset by Chris Fayers, Cardigan, Wales.
Printed and bound in Great Britain by J. W. Arrowsmith Ltd.

This book is sold subject to the condition that it shall not, by trade or otherwise, be lent, re-sold, hired out or otherwise circulated without the publisher's prior written consent in any form of binding or cover other than that in which it is published here and without a similar condition being imposed on the subsequent purchaser.

Except for short passages for review purposes, no part of this publication may be reproduced, stored in a retrieval system, or transmitted in any form, or by any means, electronic, mechanical, photocopying, recording or otherwise, without the prior written permission of Onlywomen Press Ltd.

for all at Ulverston Mind

Chapter 1

I shook the can of spray paint, and tugged a tiny damp cushion of moss from the wall I was on the brink of defacing.

"Come on Heather, don't mess me about now. You said flowing handwriting, and that's what you're getting." I took a step back, and eyed up the rough surface again. The letters should be at this height, and extend over that jagged fissure. . .

"I don't know." Her voice, still precisely Scottish after all the years down here, was thoughtful behind me, "Maybe the revolutionary style which looks like it's been written in blood would be better after all."

I gave a snarl which she couldn't see. I was cold, I was having a woozy day and didn't feel too good. Vandalising the remains of the old Berkeley Dock would never be classified as a therapeutic activity by even the most sympathetic health professional, and, sworn to secrecy, I hadn't breathed a word of my new career as a graffiti artist to my friends, Frances and Philippa, in whose outhouse I was currently squatting. They naively imagined that I was having lunch with Heather in the community centre before we went into the Art Project. I gave the can another shake,

"I thought we'd agreed it was too much of a cliché." My lips were going numb in the wind which was always fiercer in Millford than anywhere else inland, and the nasty brown clouds threatened snow, making the thready neon of the pseudo-American complex of multi-screen cinema, bowling alley, pizza chain outpost and McDonalds over to my right a place where I might actually want to be. I hit on a compromise.

"Ok, what if I do the handwriting, and a blood-drip effect from the last letter. You'll get the best of both worlds. A reference to both classical and modern politics."

I looked over my shoulder, and watched her peaky face smile

from swathes of hats, scarves and blankets.

"Och, you're a genius. Fire away, Botticelli."

I fired away. I'd practised with the can on a sheet of plywood in Heather's back garden, and the draughtsman's old meticulous care refused to desert me. I became less aware of the driving January chill, and more an arm and eye and hand, translating abstract thought into bright existence. I added some convincing runs of blood, turned round, and joined Heather, before letting myself view my handiwork as a whole.

"Fucking magic." Her better arm reached out to relieve me of the can, "Now for the rest of the installation."

I couldn't keep the satisfaction out of my voice. "Not bad is it? Maybe you were right not to ask Claire the Carer to help."

"She has enough to put up with. All the stuff should be in the bags."

I unhooked plastic carrier bags from the handles of her chair, arranged their contents on the ground to her satisfaction, and steadied her weaker arm while she used up a roll of film recording our efforts for her semi-secret portfolio.

"Perhaps I should try a few standing up. Get a different angle. Hold this a mo'." She thrust the camera into my hand.

After a year of usually undemanding association, I knew better than to say anything. I let her move her footrests and disentangle herself from her wrappings, and offered myself as a silent prop, studying our bizarre additions to this strip of raddled wasteground. My crimson letters blazed "Arma virumque cano" on the mottled wall of an abandoned building, and a battered hard hat, a pair of steel-toed boots, welder's goggles, one glove, a half-eaten meat and potato pie, a condom (fortunately unused), and a packet of cigarettes with a disposable lighter lay scattered like grave goods on a low pile of rubble.

"God, it's cold." Heather dropped back into the chair, "Let's get out of this manky hole. You can leave the condom. And the pie, I don't fancy it now."

I started chucking things into bags, "Thanks a million. I'm sure the seagulls and any passing teenager will be grateful. I hope no-one's seen us, we're not meant to be here, and writing on walls is still an offence. Take your brakes off, why don't you, it makes moving easier." I began pushing, almost jogging to force some warmth into my limbs, heading for the hole in the hoarding which screened the dock.

"That's right, tip me out in your hurry. How about passing by the bakery, I sense a vanilla slice coming on. Anyway, who's going to be heartless enough to prosecute a wheelchair-user and a nutter?" She took a last look at my writing and began laughing, "Awa wi' ye, Eamon Bannon strikes again."

I jolted her on to the safety of the pavement. Eamon Bannon, conceptual artist, was an increasingly life-size figment of her imagination, named after a football player on her home team in the eighties, and nursed gradually into existence through her months of pain and indignity. Born in an East Fife mining town, he combined working class credentials with the mind of an opinionated polymath, a fondness for cocaine and alcohol, and a contempt for anything that smacked of narrow representation. Railing against the elitism of art schools and the concept that genius could be taught, he produced challenging work which forced his audience to consider the big issues: life, death, sex, and our miniscule place in history. Or so he thought, when he wasn't partying in nightclubs, or luring page three girls to his chaotic flat in the latest undiscovered part of London. He did his serious creativity in a barn he had bought in the Welsh countryside, where he locked himself away with his brandy and his inner devils, thinking about wrapping Nelson's column in used nappies, and disguising the fact that he could actually draw. His early sketches, although tainted with a hint of pastiche, had an unexpectedly charming directness and vigour, and told of an almost lyrical side to his tormented drive. I should know, I had done them myself, and was especially proud of the drawing of his mother, filling in a pools coupon at the kitchen table.

When I met Heather, on my first shaky visit to the Art Project, she already had most of Eamon's biography in place, and after a few weeks had ear-marked me as a likely collaborator in her mission to sell Eamon's work to an influential advertising executive and art-collector in London. She had watched me on about ten per cent capacity automatically helping William in his effort to make a horse gallop across a winter landscape, laughing in spite of myself at May trying to explain tactfully to Gladys that her silk-painted bullrush looked like a vibrator.

"You know, lass, those things that modern girls use when they need a man."

"A dating agency?"

Out of the corner of my eye, I saw the newspaper shake in Heather's hands.

"That's everybody's horoscopes," she said, a catch in her voice. "If I make you a cuppa, Sarah, will you wheel me out for a wee smoke?"

I was surprised at her invitation: she had been pleasant enough, although not particularly forthcoming so far; yet she endured my clumsiness in heaving her out of the door with good grace, and smiled when I came back with the two mugs of coffee she couldn't carry.

"Ta, hen. We should get some tubs of flowers and stuff for here in the summer. Tart the old place up a bit."

I looked around. The back yard of the community centre was grim, and we smokers huddled in the roofed corner where the bins were kept. After quitting when I was twenty, I had cultivated a fifteen a day habit in the hospital, and was not likely to stop again soon.

"It's still better than the smoke room at Monk's House," I said, so that she would be under no illusions over where I had come from.

"Aye, so I've heard." She smiled again, "I wouldn't go in. Even they had the sense to see I didn't have a mental health problem, only a life ruined problem."

I raised an eyebrow, and waited to see if she would tell me more.

"Car smash. Some barmpot hit me head on and killed himself. When I came home from hospital the first time, I took every pill in the house, and I had quite a collection." She watched the smoke spiralling from her nostrils. "Then my neighbour found me." She laughed, "He's a drug dealer, and probably wanted to see if I had anything surplus to requirements. But he did the decent thing, the bastard, and I'm still here today. What about you?"

There was no point in being evasive. "I went mad," I said succinctly.

"Yeah, well, that goes without saying, seeing you were in Monk's House. How mad?"

"Pretty mad." I smiled back at her, "They say it's depression, but I was definitely loopy loo until the pills started working, and I'm not sure how sane I am now."

"You don't seem too nuts to me. You're an artist, aren't you?"

I scuffled my feet. "I was a cartoonist before." Now I wasn't anything, and would never draw those highly-praised satirical strips for gay publications again.

"Right." She drew on her cigarette, "Modern art's shite, isn't it?"

"We-ell. . ."

"Aw, gie us a break. All those piles of junk and crappy videos. Anyone with an idea and a wee bitty technical skill could do it. How're you on keeping confidences?"

That was when she introduced me to Eamon, and through the year persuaded me, against what was left of my better judgement, to accompany her on expeditions to create Eamon's "installations", which she then religiously photographed. I had placed police "Accident Here" signs in spring woodland, decorated the beach in summer with kippers from the supermarket, and propped a collage of explicit nudes in a hedge glowing with autumn berries. She explained solemnly that the work in Berkeley Dock would complete the seasonal cycle, and that Eamon might move on to something new. We discussed the possibilities over vanilla slices in the cafe attached to the bakery.

"Models," she said indistinctly through flaky pastry and confectioner's custard. "I think he's decided to work on a more intimate scale. Papier-mache's an interesting medium."

I looked at her, "Jesus. What do you want me to do now? Raid the council recycling bins for raw materials?"

When she giggled like this, I forgot that I'd wheeled her in, and that she wasn't going to skip out of the door in front of me. Heather was beautiful. She kept her thick black wavy hair at shoulder length, her eyes were deep blue, and her high-boned features told of ancestors who had run up and down highland glens before the clearances forced them to Dundee. Added to this, she was horribly clever, and still did odd freelance jobs for the firm of solicitors in which she'd been a partner, on top of acting as an unpaid legal advisor to a wide circle of neighbours, their friends, and anyone else whose problems could divert her. More than one runaway husband or wife had thought twice about being awkward with their deserted partner when they found out that Heather was on their case, and since she had never shopped anyone to the social for engaging in all the entrepreneurial activities vital to people for whom long-term employment was a fantasy, she was more or less trusted on her patch. She bought eggs from the couple who kept hens on their allotment, used the local mechanic to fix her car, and was in demand to be present at the interviews with officialdom which plagued the lives of those around her.

"What can they do to me?" she asked rhetorically, "I'm a fucking prisoner already. The benefits system assumes that everyone's dishonest anyway, and until they change their attitude and give human beings some respect and enough to live on, I see nothing immoral in wringing what I can out of it for my pals. Any time they try and tell you that you're cured, I'll be there, swearing you're on a knife edge, no worries."

"A model pig with its side cut out to show a string of sausages inside," she suggested at the Art Project door. "We'll get some old sausages from the market, and inject them with formaldehyde. Whippy can lay his hands on some I'm sure."

Whippy was her drug-dealer neighbour, and the source of most of her props.

I held the door open, so that she could propel herself through, "You should have saved that pie. It could have gone in a model cow."

Gladys saw us and pointed a pencil at me, "There she is, the idle bugger. Draw me a rabbit, I've been waiting since dinner time."

Bridie waved an illustrated book in front of Heather. "Easter, girls. How about a range of cards with matching ornamental eggs? And Valentine's Day, we must exploit it this year. There's a craft fair the weekend before, we'll book a table."

I hung up my coat, and winked at Gladys, "The reward of patience is patience. What kind of rabbit do you want? And I'm not doing padded red hearts with lace on," I added to Bridie, "I have my standards."

"Yeah, pretty damn low ones. Put the kettle on, there's a love, I've got to finish these curtains for that Mrs Whatsit." She selected a pair of spectacles from the three which hung on cords round her neck, "Where did I put those scissors?"

I found the scissors, made cups of tea and coffee, drew a revoltingly cute rabbit for Gladys, and hemmed curtains for Bridie, who had been distracted by Heather's idea that we should compose unique verses for our Valentine's cards.

"Roses are red, violets are blue, when I get frisky, I think of you," May said po-faced.

William went red and stood up. "There's more hot air coming from you women than from the radiators. I'm off to get the paper. Who wants sweets?" He took orders for mints and chocolate bars, and stomped off on his regular afternoon errand.

I folded the curtains, and felt better. The Art Project had been a life-saver. Starting off as little more than a large room with basic materials in the community centre, under Bridie's direction it was now a hub of individual and group activity. On two afternoons a week, she presided over those who wanted to paint quietly in a corner, those who were willing to join her in making items to sell to buy more equipment, and pensioners like May, Gladys and William, who really wanted company and a good chat.

"I rule this place with a rod of iron," she had lied on my initial visit, "and I don't pass anything on to that Maggie at the hospital unless you tell me I can."

That part at least was the truth. I had gathered that Maggie, an occupational therapist attached to the Monk's House Acute Psychiatric Unit, had been involved in setting up the Art Project, and she had steered me in its direction when Frances and Philippa had demanded that the Unit should provide me with my statutory right to a care programme on my discharge. What had seemed like a necessary safety net gradually became a millstone, as I trotted dutifully off to dull discussion groups, stress-inducing relaxation classes and meetings with staff who filled in reams of politically correct forms. Only the Art Project, free from the stifling right-on language of the professionals, had engaged my interest. Bridie, for all her boundless patience and good humour, never fixed anyone with a compassionate stare and murmured, "How does that make you feel?" or "That was very brave of you to be so honest in sharing." She just rambled on in her stream of consciousness manner, and set you to finding her handbag, which she lost several times a day, or asked for your advice on her latest diet. As tall as me, and a lot heavier, she refused to be consoled by our collective assertions that men didn't like skinny women who looked as if they would break in two if they tried to have sex.

"I'm such a blimp, though," she would moan, "sometimes I think I'll never do it again," and the conversation would deteriorate into a discussion of the pros and cons of having a sex life.

This afternoon, she was on one of her fresh fruit kicks, and ostentatiously crunched an apple while William distributed goodies and counted out change.

"Sad news, I'm afraid," he said, unfolding the evening paper. "They identified that body on South Beach. Must have been a suicide." He glanced at me, "He was in Monk's House over a year back. Sorry to be the one to tell you if you knew him, but you'll read it yourself anyway."

Like most older people in Millford, William believed that everyone read the Millford Gazette from cover to cover over their tea.

My fists clenched slightly, "What was his name?"

William followed the newsprint with one thick finger, "Hang on, here it is. Hall, David Hall."

"Shit." I reached for my cigarettes. "Yeah, I knew him. He was in for about two weeks. He worked for the Borough Council, he was nice." My voice tailed away. Bridie put a hand on my arm, and I listened to the others speculating out loud on whether it could have been an accident, the tides were terrible at this time of year, remember that couple who had drowned trying to save their dog, and May's cousin's husband who had only been saved by the coastguard, and what happened to those lifebelts they used to have along the road by the beach?

"All right?" Bridie asked quietly.

I recalled the gentle man who had forced himself not to cry after his grandchildren had visited the unit, and who had played the meanest game of Scrabble I had ever come across.

"Yup. I'm nipping out for a smoke."

The clouds were releasing snow at last, and I stuck my head out of the shelter to look up at the whirling grey flakes, and feel their stinging melt on my warm cheeks. David would never see another snowfield sparkling in the sun, or the crocuses coming through in the spring. I tried to be sad, and felt only rage and the dark thump of fear. He hadn't been half as bad as me, and if he could lose it and give way to the urge to enter the lumpy unforgiving water, what chance would I have in the end? He'd been in the hospital for depression, why had they let him get so ill again? Where had his care in the community and the multi-disciplinary mental health team been? On paper, that's where, in the fine mission statements crafted in management meetings, where the stark reality of underpaid, overworked, off-on-the-sick staff rarely intruded. His GP might have ignored his pleas that his medication wasn't working, he might have tried to see a community nurse, and been told that there was a two month waiting list, he might have been turned away from A and E by a locum who wouldn't recognise a clinical depression if it jumped up and hit him over the head with a chair. I betted that with no one in the know to back him up, he had never been told that he was entitled to a care programme. The bitter anger which had sustained me into recovery set my jaw, and sent my cigarette end spinning into the snow. It wasn't good enough. I would find out who had failed him and why, and make such a noise over this one unnecessary death that the inert system would move, and start to save lives instead of wasting them. I resisted the temptation to scream up at the sky, and stamped inside, an avenging angel with chilly feet.

Chapter 2

I ranted to Heather and Bridie by the kettle, and became calmer, if no less determined. Discovering that my heart wasn't pounding nor my mind rushing with the overwhelming thoughts which could herald a relapse, I bought my own newspaper on the way to the bus stop, and even enjoyed the crunch of settling snow under my feet. In the bus shelter, I joined the communal moaning about the weather, and once the bus had arrived, ten minutes late, savoured its warm stink of fuel oil and old upholstery. Rivulets of melted snow dribbled down the centre aisle, and the driver struggled with flapping wipers and wiseass passengers.

"Hope you've got a spade for when we get stuck."

"If you fetch up in a snowdrift, make sure it's outside the Carters' Arms."

Cars were driving slowly on the outskirts of town, and the windows went black and cold when we hit the back lanes through the villages. My paper was already soggy, and the headline, "Call Centre Bosses To Visit Millford", was losing its bold crispness. I didn't particularly want to read the latest about the Borough Council's insane belief that a call centre was the answer to all Millford's problems, and made myself turn to the side column, which informed me that the body found yesterday on South Beach, Trotters Bank, had been identified as that of David Hall, formerly of the Borough Council Treasury Department, who had been undergoing treatment for depression for the past two years. It didn't fail to mention that this treatment had included a spell in Monk's House Acute Psychiatric Unit. The implication was clear. Here was another sad case of a disturbed soul, who, beyond help, had decided to end it all, and who didn't merit as many inches as the woman who had come across a drawing pin in a pot of yoghurt, which was the engrossing subject of the third article on the front page. "I was shocked and upset," she was reported to have said, "I dread to think what could have happened if a kiddie had swallowed it. I always buy my yoghurts from the same shop, and you don't expect this kind of thing nowadays." I guessed that in a few days' time, the headline would be "Yoghurt Trauma Woman Seeks Compensation", and wondered if she herself had popped the pin in. As long as it wasn't for being charged with theft or drunken affray, most of us here were very partial to having our names published in the Gazette. For all I knew, though, being named and shamed in the paper for fighting whilst under the influence might be a desirable badge of adulthood for young Millford men, a rite of passage necessary to attain the respect of the male community, like a warrior's initiation in Papua New Guinea. I pondered. If I was a straight Millford girl, would I prefer a boyfriend who would throw a punch at someone who tried to cop off with me on a Friday night, or a partner who merely crossed his eyes, and sank to the floor in an alcoholic stupor?

The bus coming to a careful halt at the bus stop in Byreby village ended my musing, and I began the trek down a mile of rutted lane to Frances' and Philippa's house. It was a walk I had done so often, that sometimes I could arrive home without any recollection of my brisk stroll between neglected hedges, and I would realise that I had ploughed past opening buds or first flowers with no pause for appreciation. Tonight was different, and my tramp felt more like a doomed Siberian expedition than a necessary exercise which had to be accomplished as quickly as possible. Snow stuck to my coat and legs, infiltrating the gaps at my collar and cuffs, and when I stood still, I could hear nothing but its whispering descent and the clack of bare branches in the wind. Some evenings there was an owl in the ash tree which marked the half-way point of the track, and once or twice I had caught sight of a huddled shape perched on a high bough, but today his eerie call was absent, and I was the only breathing thing moving through the murk.

"Jesus Christ, girl," I told myself, "you could have driven into town." If I tripped and broke my ankle, how long would it be before Frances and Philippa worked out that something was amiss, and sent out a search party to save me from hypothermia? Probably not until after the Archers, which usually meant supper time. Sustained by this cheerful thought, I kept grimly on until I saw the wobbly outside light which marked the gable end of Frances' workshop, the former barn attached to their old farmhouse. I staggered round it, into the yard at the back, past Philippa's tool store and spare greenhouse, and onwards to the detached washhouse, which was my palatial abode. One day, Frances and Philippa were going to dig out the century's worth of impacted mud in the yard, and find the lovely cobbled surface they were convinced lurked below, but until then, I had to contend with an approach to my front door that resembled a miniature working model of the Western Front. My legs failing, I fell inside like a weary yeti, and reached for the solitary light switch.

As the long-life bulb gathered strength, I saw a discreet pile of rucked-up Indian bedspread and bald towel on my settee give a little writhe, and a pink and brown snout emerge. It would be pleasant to record that Curlydog had eagerly awaited my arrival, and jumped up to cover me with the unconditional love that is the preserve of faithful dogs, but she did nothing of the sort. She crawled groaning from her carefully arranged nest, and gave me a cursory wag of the peculiarly bent tail which gave her her name. She sniffed at my wet boots, jumped at the water dripping from my coat, and looked dubiously at the door.

"Go and have a pee, useless guard dog," I told her, and shoved her barrel body outside.

By the time I had kicked off my boots and coat, and was coaxing my stove into life, a fierce scratching on the door told me she had had enough, and she shot in, more friendly now, to shake in front of the fire and ask me beseechingly if I was ever going to feed her. A mixed up terrier of indeterminate age, with a short brindled white and brown coat, she had come to me through a friend of Philippa's who, seeing her at the Animal Rescue shelter, had jumped to the conclusion that bonding with an abandoned mongrel would be the key to my recovery. We had treated each other with polite suspicion for a few weeks, and then she had tested my commitment by disappearing down a rabbit hole while I was trying to make her accompany me on a jog. My frantic calling, and attempts to dig her out with a spade borrowed from a phlegmatically amused farmer, must have convinced her that I was worth keeping on, and after that we worked out a mutually satisfying mode of cohabiting. If I stopped forcing her to jog with me, she would curb her natural instinct to run off, and if I tolerated her nesting habits, she would spend less time calculating how to open cupboard doors to steal food. At heart, she was a simple soul, who enjoyed sleeping, eating, pottering around the yard, the occasional rat hunt and tormenting Doris and Ethel, Philippa's cats, with her uncouth ways. Doris and Ethel lived lives governed by rules of precedence as complex as those of a Hapsburg court, with their days structured by elaborate rituals around feeding bowls, favourite chairs, and the prime position in the airing cupboard. They watched in disbelief as Curlydog galloped roughshod through all accepted etiquette, and they spent hours together on the kitchen windowsill, spying through the glass on my door, and plotting how to ambush this barbaric interloper if she came out. One sunny Spring afternoon last year, intrigued by these three's manoueverings around walls and over rooftops, I had found myself scrabbling for paper and pencil, and a couple of hours later, with a mixture of surprise and alarm, discovered that I had drawn four pages of cartoons, complete with speech bubbles. By now, over nine months later, I had almost a book's worth, and the cast had expanded to include Philippa's herd of ferocious bantams in their pen beyond the vegetable garden, the frogs in her pond, and a handsome labrador from the village, with whom Curlydog shamelessly flirted on his frequent escapes from his garden and visits to us. Like Eamon Bannon, I had kept these to myself, since I wasn't sure if there was a market for a cartoon soap opera, whose over-sexed and badly behaved characters were domestic and garden animals. I was convinced that my former agent, who still occasionally badgered me to start producing again, would not take kindly to my change of direction. Besides, my living arrangements, even more than my stay in Monk's House, had deepened her belief that I had permanently lost my marbles.

She had been bemused, and I had been pathetically grateful, when Frances and Philippa had taken over while, lost in the profound conviction that I would never again be well enough to come out, I was existing in the hospital. I had told them seriously over the phone that they could dispose of all my belongings because I was going to let the bank repossess my house, since the fact that I would never work again obviously meant that I could not pay the mortgage, and would they please fetch me the paperwork from the bank so that I could cancel my standing orders and let my debts mount up. They had sensibly ignored me, moved my personal possessions to the washhouse which they had recently re-roofed and damp-proofed, and rented out my house to a nice couple with a toddler and another on the way.

"There's no way you can live on your own when you come out," Philippa had informed me on one of their many visits, "but we've given them a proper lease renewable every six months, so if you want to go back at some point you can."

"So where. . .?"

They both looked at me as if I had asked an exceptionally dim question, and Frances crushed her can from the soft drinks machine with barely a movement of her broad, broken-nailed hand.

"With us, pea brain. Unless you find somewhere else you'd prefer."

Seemingly unaware that they had saved my life, and were continuing to do so with no apparent time limit to their humane generosity, they had absorbed me into their routine, as they had previously absorbed Frances' nephew who had once run away from home for a month, and Young Adam, Philippa's assistant in her gardening business, who one winter had needed a temporary refuge from his noisy step-brothers. I had slept in their attic, fragrant with stored apples and bunches of dried herbs hanging from uneven beams, until the February afternoon which I had resolved to spend squaring up to the piled boxes and suitcases in the washhouse. In the process of making the washhouse weatherproof, Frances had put in a stove made from an old-fashioned milk churn, and, pursing her lips at my indifference to comfort, she had lit it and stoked it up for the afternoon with off-cuts from her workshop.

"Need to see if it smokes anyway," she had grunted, "let me know," and she had returned to carving the highly-prized furniture she made to order.

After a desultory poke at a few suitcases, I staved off my black despair at the lost lifestyle of labels and city clubs they invoked by flicking through a book of wood-engravings I used to keep handy in my sitting room, mainly, it has to be said, to impress the overnight visitors whom I attracted back from those clubs. The stove, drawing cleanly, belted out heat, I gazed at a picture of horses ploughing a long gone field, and, frail as a down feather, the minutest intimation of peace touched my heart. "I could live here." The words popped in and out of my head, and I had to acknowledge that for five precious minutes, I had been clear of the constant thought that I was on the verge of tipping once more into insanity.

Neither Frances nor Philippa raised any objections to my suggestion, and by the end of the week, I was installed. The bed came down from the attic to be replaced by my suitcases, I scoured the Millford charity shops for rugs, odd sticks of furniture and a velvet curtain to screen off a bedroom, and bodged up a sink, which I fed from a tank propped on a stand I made myself, and drained through a rusty pipe into a soakaway Frances and I dug outside the back wall. I cleared out the still-functioning outside loo in the yard, mixed together all the half-tins of off-white paint stored in the back pantry, and slapped the results on my interior walls. On my last official day in the main house, I found my old track suit and trainers, and, before I could talk myself out of it, had pulled them on and was running round the lanes. At the farthest point from the house, I bent double by a gate, at the very end of my physical limits. Pouring with sweat, thighs like lead, heart-rate in the danger zone, I had a massive coughing fit which sent sheep bounding for cover. Somehow I teetered bow-legged home, where I went upstairs on all fours so that I could at least expire in the comfort of a hot bath. Frances came in from her workshop to find me by the Rayburn, speechless with fatigue and draped in Doris and Ethel.

"Jesus God, you look like a real person again," she muttered, and clomped off to clog up the shower with sawdust.

That was all either of them said about this apparent turning point in my fortunes, and although I'd had horrible days and foul nights since, day by day I thought less and less of an imminent return to the hospital, and the massed mightmare clouds of terror and illness sank lower and lower beneath my personal horizon.

I still hadn't foreseen that, almost a year later, I would be the proud owner of a dog, a much fitter body, and a mind which didn't go haywire at the news that someone I knew had died. I told Curlydog about David after she had gobbled her supper and was hiccupping on my lap, and she responded with a sympathetic, if foul-breathed, attempt to lick my face. At least Frances and Philippa, although they were equally sympathetic in their different ways, refrained from a similar gesture.

"Oh dear," Frances said vaguely from the corner where she was reading the classified ads in my paper.

Philippa gave her special chilli sauce a quick stir, and threw pasta erratically into a pan. "That's appalling. Why wasn't anyone taking care of him? Poor, poor man. Did he live on Trotters Bank? Or do you think he went out there specially? I hope the hospital and everyone else are ashamed of themselves, you're right, you should make a fuss and give them all a kick up the arse. Write to the health authority and our MP, I'll help, get a pen this minute, Fran, and I'll dictate."

Frances buried her head further into the sports pages. As taciturn as Philippa was voluble, she had an enviable ability to filter out the tasks Philippa genuinely wanted to be performed from her daily barrage of instructions and schemes. She murmured something that sounded like, "Should check with family first."

"You're so sensible." Philippa whacked bread on to the table.

"Doris, Ethel, which one of you has been licking the butter?" They casually averted their heads while she scraped off the minute grooved marks with a knife. "Any more of this, and I'll make you live in the back pantry all winter. And stop blaming it on Curlydog, the poor lamb has been shut up in her own house since midday."

Curlydog looked smug, and the cats, preening in front of the Rayburn, pretended she wasn't there. They knew that one day she would be caught red-handed in a daring food theft, and were prepared to bide their time.

"Well?" Philippa returned to the matter in hand. "Did David Hall have any family that you know of? Where do they live? Locally or away?"

I dredged my brain for memories I had tried to blank off. "He had a son, who's married with children. I think they all lived on Trotters Bank."

"There you go. Get in touch with this son, and get the lowdown. He'll be in the phone book. At least they're not from the Sink, not that it would make any difference, of course."

I grinned, "Of course."

The Sink was the name generations of Millford people had given to a slum parcel of Victorian workers' housing in the heart of the old docks system. Rumours abounded that the Borough Council, having renamed this socially excluded area Merchants' Wharf, had banned all its employees from so much as whispering its accepted name, and had secretly threatened the Gazette with writs if the word ever appeared in its columns. Everyone else treated the Council's pretensions with the contempt they deserved, in much the same way as they persisted in calling the magnificently refurbished "Onshore Leisure Centre and Spa" the Borough Baths, and Admiral Street, with its late-night bars and clubs, the Reeperbahn. Trotters Bank, the long, thin island a few hundred yards off Millford, and joined to the town by an ugly concrete bridge, was generally accepted as a separate world. Its original inhabitants, claiming Viking ancestry, maintained that its name derived from the Norse God, Thor, while those on the mainland believed that it was a corruption of Traitors' Bank, since its unruly natives, at some suitably vague moment in history, had behaved with unspeakable treachery. Depending upon who was telling you, this treachery consisted of paying tribute to the Scots, sheltering survivors from the Spanish Armada, turning a cannon on one of Nelson's frigates to deter the press-gang, smuggling slaves after Abolition, or sabotaging warships in Millford during the Great War. Both sides energetically refuted any presumptuous local historian's claim that an eighteenth-century landowner called Trotter had named the island after himself, and kept this minor feud simmering to provide entertainment when times were dull. Together with a subterranean sectarianism, it was one of the divisions which bound a population descended from the migrants who had flocked to Millford less than a hundred and fifty years ago and created a large working town where there had previously been twelve fisher cottages and a ruined convent.

As if it was settled that I should pursue David's son, over supper Philippa gave us her considered thoughts about the weather, and how it would affect her plans for putting me and the rest of the county to work.

"I suppose Adam and I could possibly carry on hacking Dr Grey's shrubbery about tomorrow, though it'll be a bit cold and wet if the snow keeps sticking. On the other hand, the gritters might have been out, and we can drive over to that potter in Yorkshire and pick up those planters for Mrs Scott-Wilson. What's this snow going to do, Fran? Get worse, stay the same, freeze or melt?"

Frances was our oracle on the weather. Until she had met Philippa, she had lived in a tepee in a damp valley, and probably had fifty private words for different types of rain.

"Thaw by tomorrow afternoon," she said, and let Ethel jump up to her knee, so she could see what we were eating.

"You don't like chilli, Fuzzyface," Philippa said indulgently, then turned to me. "You still won't be able to work on that wall. You'll have to help Frances if she can use you."

Frances smiled under her dark eyebrows, "Lots of polishing waiting for you."

I pulled a nasty face. "Wonderful. I hurt my wrist today."

She made a doorstop disappear with hardly a gulp. "No you didn't. We'll be able to get our squash game in as well. Six o'clock. I booked the court."

"Bite her ankles, Curlydog. Can't I do something nice and restful in the greenhouses?"

"Nuh huh." Frances ambled to the Rayburn to put the kettle on. "Tomorrow you're all mine."

I really wasn't mad about polishing, but my protests were little more than acting. Frances and Philippa had refused my offers of rent for the washhouse, claiming that any other source of income would push filling in their tax forms beyond the boundaries of complicated into the realms of the unbearable, and so I gave them three days a week of free labour instead. Philippa, who had never had enough time to whip her vegetable garden into shape, was delighted, and I had discovered an unexpected sense of achievement in helping to produce beautiful rows of edible greenery. Frances' craft demanded far more skill than that needed for digging, weeding, throwing manure around, and transplanting, and all she could offer me was polishing finished articles and the occasional trip to her suppliers or customers. This winter, after a few lessons from Young Adam, I had been occupied in slowly rebuilding the dry stone wall which bounded the garden, and I knew that heaving stones would distract me from gnawing at the tragedy of David's death far more than trying to give chairs a professional sheen. Still, Frances would be quiet, yet reassuring company, and I held the prospect of our weekly squash battle up as a talisman against the army of bleak thoughts waiting to attack once I was back in the washhouse and alone. In bed, I clutched at the quilt, concentrating on the sounds of logs subsiding in the stove and Curlydog's contented breathing. Striving to take a few more points off Frances was a better option than letting myself feel the ultimate futility of all human endeavour, and anyway, who else could conspire with Heather in launching Eamon Bannon on an unsuspecting art world? Arguing furiously with myself that I was nowhere near to taking David's route out of this weary existence, I waited for sleep to come.

Chapter 3

I admired and respected many facets of Frances' character. Her artistry and originality in her craft, her proven ability to live comfortably and productively for years in conditions which I would consider unendurably primitive, and her deep love for Philippa, which had overridden her objections to residing in a conventional house with running water, a washing machine and regular baths. However, her behaviour on the squash court fell well outside this category of virtues. On paper, I had all the advantages, being taller, slimmer, fitter and far more agile, yet this counted for nothing in dealing with a creature possessed of ferocious competitiveness and odious cunning. The minute she walked through the court door, squat and baggy in her unfashionable shorts, she turned into a vicious troll, whose only purpose was to beat me into a humiliated pulp. Her normal amiable expression was replaced with a mask of dreadful concentration, her everyday taciturnity changed into monosyllabic curtness, and growls of fury met any foolish attempt I made to question her version of the score. After the shock of our first match, which was so far removed from the friendly knock about I'd been expecting that I wondered if I'd lost contact with reality again, I'd set myself the goal of finding weaknesses in her game, and gradually learning to exploit them, so that one day I would scrape a victory. It wasn't going to happen soon, and our match the next day followed the usual pattern. When it was over, she wiped the solitary bead of sweat from her brow, and pulled me up from where I lay in the corner.

"Good game. You only hit the wall twice."

"Piss off."

"Bet it stopped you agitating about David though. More than the polishing, anyway."

"Was it that obvious?"

Although I had tried to polish conscientiously all day, I had been unable to quell the anxiety fogging my mind's edges and making me drop tins of polish with monotonous regularity.

"Yeah. A nice shower, and you'll be back to normal."

She was mostly right. Pink and glowing, I sat on the changing room bench, pulling on my socks, only half aware of the noisy group of women who'd been having a five-a-side football and profanity match.

"You were taking the piss with those tackles, Warren. Violence is no substitute for technique."

"Up your arse."

"You wish, sweetheart."

Waves of laughter broke on the steamy walls. I guessed that I'd be no better at football than I was at squash, and reached for my jeans. At least my legs were nicer than Frances', and my stomach against the buttons was almost flat. I swayed my hips to a full length mirror, and flicked a comb at my short, blonde-ish hair. Let's face it, I was pretty damn gorgeous these days. Frances nudged me, not very discreetly.

"Don't look now. That one called Warren is staring at you."

I looked. My chest tightened with something like fear and disappointment. Maggie, the occupational therapist from Monk's House, was giving me a professional smile. I sent her a brief grimace in return, stuffed gear into my bag, picked up my racquet, and made for the door.

"Too hot in here. I'll wait for you in the lobby," I hissed out of the corner of my mouth at Frances, and raced past the footballers, my eyes fixed on the door handle. It shouldn't still be happening, I told myself as I pretended to read notices in the reception area, this feeling that I had done something very wrong, and had been found out, which continued to hit me whenever I ran into any Monk's House staff in shops or on the street. You're normal now, you're as entitled to be here at the Borough Baths with your friend as they are, don't be wet. Where the hell was Frances? She must have found an acquaintance to chat to, because when the changing room door opened and closed again, it was Maggie of all people who was strolling towards me. Her smile hadn't slipped.

"Hi there. All right?"

I thought I caught the therapist's false empathy in her voice, and was suddenly angry.

"Not too bad. At least I'm alive, not like some of your patients."

Jesus, whatever had possessed me to come out with that? She'd diagnose a crisis on the spot, and have me inside before you could say Mental Health Act.

"What?" She came to a halt, nearly rocking on her heels, as if I'd smacked her.

I back-pedalled, and felt my cooling face re-ignite with a shameful blush.

"Sorry, it's not you. David Hall dying, I was with him in the hospital, I saw it in the Gazette. Can't help feeling that the system let him down, didn't help him if he was getting ill again. He should have had a care programme to support him. . ."

I was mumbling, and inching backwards towards the main exit. I would run out, and hide behind Frances' van.

Her face stiffened. "Ah. Yes, of course. We're all very sad about him. I think we did all we could for him, you know."

Now she didn't bother to disguise her detached sympathy, and I was childishly angry again.

"Well, you have to say that, don't you. Doesn't exactly inspire me with confidence for my future all the same. Let's hope I'm one of the lucky one in ten people who don't have a relapse, eh?"

At long last, Frances had emerged from the changing room, and was hanging back, smirking horribly.

"Just how many ex-patients have to drown themselves, before you lot take depression seriously?"

I threw in the best parting shot I could manage in the circumstances, and bolted outside.

"Get her mobile number, did you?" Frances asked heartlessly, catching up with me in the car park.

I stepped into a puddle, soaking my warm, clean feet. Frances' thaw had arrived as forecast.

"Aagh fuck!" I jumped up and down in rage and embarrassment. "No, I had a go at her. She works at Monk's House, she must think I'm a total. . .arsewit, loser, aggressive paranoic."

"All in a day's work to her," Frances said comfortably. "Chips on the way home?"

"You said what to Maggie Warren?" Bridie hooted the following afternoon at the Art Project.

"I asked her how many of her patients had to drown themselves before she took them seriously," I giggled. The previous night's exercise and a generous dose of fats and carbohydrate had done the trick, and I was back in my hard won equilibrium.

"Good for you lass," May put her oar in from the sewing machine. "A little trouble with our nerves, and they think we were born yesterday."

"All that university education, and they haven't an ounce of common sense," Heather fanned May's flames.

May dived willingly into one of her illogical diatribes against the shortcomings of the modern health service, and I bent my head over a sketch pad. Valentine's Day. I started on a chubby Cupid with a face a bit like Bridie's.

May eventually ran out of steam, and came to take a look on her way to the kettle.

"Ooh, that's nice, aren't you clever." She put a hand on her bosom, "Cupid, draw back your bo-ow..." She had a powerful singing voice for her age.

We joined in, and were on assorted woo-woo-woos, when the door opened.

"Choir practice?" Maggie Warren's head peered in at us. This was unfair, I had avoided her for nearly a year, and now she had materialised twice in two days.

"It's the boss," May shrieked, "we're undone, girls."

"Yeah." Maggie stepped in, "I've been studying the productivity figures for this project, and they're nowhere near good enough. Profits, I need profits." She thumped her fist on a table, "How else am I going to afford my holidays in Barbados?" She had hit the right note with May, who laughed with her, her animosity forgotten.

Bridie tried to look efficient. "Cup of tea, dear? Was it the health and safety report you wanted? It's in my bag." I saw that her fingers were crossed behind her back.

Maggie covered her mouth with her hand. "Oops, I'd forgotten. I'll pick it up next week, there's no point me sending yours upstairs until I've done mine, which I haven't. No," she grinned at me, "I'm a woman on a mission. I need to find an artist, and I've got my beady eye on Sarah. Can you spare me a few minutes? I'll buy you a cake in the community caff."

"You're lying," I said to myself, "you want to caution me for mouthing off to you at the Borough Baths last night."

Bridie moved protectively closer to me, "We're in the middle of something..."

"It's ok." I stood up, "That might work with some glitter on pink card." I stiffly followed Maggie out into the corridor, imagining the speculation which would bubble up the minute we were out of earshot.

Maggie led the way to the small cafe area, chattering brightly.

"I'm glad that snow's gone. It may look pretty, but it doesn't half bugger up the roads. You live out of town, don't you? Do you ever get snowed in? I was, two years ago, and had to ski to the bus stop. Then it melted, and I felt such a prat getting on the bus in the evening, looking like I'd lost the way to St Moritz. Only coffee? Sure you don't want one of these squishy buns? This table all right?"

I sat down opposite her, and waited for her to switch into ogre mode. I'd never noticed those tiny streaks of grey in her brown curls before, or that her nose was tilted up at the end.

"Oh for heaven's sake." She stuffed half a chelsea bun into her mouth and spoke around the bulge, "Relax. I'm not going to get at you for last night. Sorry about the hamster impression, I didn't have time for lunch." She gave a little moan, "These are so nice, I might have to have another."

I ventured a half smile, "Better than the vanilla slices at Benn's?"

She licked icing from the corner of her mouth, "Oh no. But I save them for Fridays for a special treat, otherwise I'd be down there every day to feed my addiction. Mind you," she pressed a fingertip on to an escaped currant, "almond slices are my real joy, I just can't seem to find any that hit the spot in Millford."

I sipped my coffee, hoping that my throat wouldn't go into spasm as it sometimes did in times of stress.

"No, pie and peas are more in the Millford line than effete cakes."

"Too right." A common interest having been established, she drew a decisive breath. I braced myself.

"Look, Sarah, this isn't why I came to find you, but I'll tell you anyway, though I probably shouldn't." She squinted into the middle distance and sighed. "David Hall didn't come to any of the groups I run, so I didn't know him. I was bugged by what you said though, and did some checking this morning." Her cheeks went red, "I'm not going to give you a load of bullshit about what a caring best practice wonk I am. I do my job. You're an intelligent, articulate woman, you know how flawed the system is, and how people can slip through the net, no matter how hard we try to patch up the gaps. The thing is," she looked directly at me, and I saw the tiny frown above her nose, "David Hall wasn't one of those, from what I gathered. His daughter-in-law is a nurse, and she saw to it that he was discharged with a proper care programme. He was an outpatient for ages, and still saw a community worker. Everyone knew what the signs of a relapse were, and so did he, he wasn't a fool. I can't give you any details, but I can say that his death was unexpected."

I was glad she didn't shy away from the "D" word, and tried to think. She leaned forward earnestly,

"His family believe that he drowned accidentally, and I don't buy that they're indulging in wishful thinking. That's the most likely explanation from what I've heard. Please believe me, I'm not saying this to get us off the hook, we make plenty of mistakes. I just want things to be clear between us."

"Oh." I was frowning back into her serious eyes. Why was she so bothered about what I thought?

"Um, why. . .?"

"Ah." Her expression cleared, and her shoulders relaxed, "I wasn't lying. I'm in urgent need of someone who can draw and paint. D'you want a job?"

"Er," I was aware of my eyes narrowing. "What sort of job?"

"Artistic consultant on Mission Muriel."

"Mission Muriel?" This woman was odder than I thought.

"I'll explain. Let me get you another coffee first. Dash of milk, two sugars?"

She was observant too. I wondered how much she knew about me. She'd most likely seen my medical records, and I cringed inside.

"Well, ta."

I eyed her surreptitiously as she dragged a smile from the volunteer behind the counter. She was shorter than me, which wasn't unusual, older, probably in her forties, and a little bit plump. Dressed in unremarkable working clothes of a long grey skirt and a jumper in a subdued pattern, she was like any other middling class member of the caring professions, with easy conversation and an internal wall to bar entry to clients who wanted a piece of her outside working hours. Maybe the football made her slightly more interesting, but that was all. I remained on my guard.

She came back, and started on her second bun.

"I'd better tell you, Mission Muriel is only my pet name for this project. Its official title is far too full of the right catchphrases. To cut a long story short," she chewed briskly, "the main hospital has a stretch of wall it wants cheering up with a mural. To soothe the troubled breasts of patients and staff alike, since it's on the way to cancer outpatients. I've bullied a group of Monk's House outpatients to sign up to work on this mural, and I had an art teacher from the college all lined up to help, since my group all swear that they can't draw for toffee. Now," she gave me a pleading look, "the whole thing, for which I've spent months doing ridiculous risk assessments and begging for materials, is likely to go belly-up because the art teacher's pulled out at the last minute. I've seen your work over the years, I'm a fan, and I bet you can paint, having been to art college and..."

"A fan?" I said, a startled squeak in my voice. I had believed that appreciation of my work was confined to lesbian circles.

"Duh." Suddenly she was completely open. "You must know. Everyone else does. I've chased after enough nurses to make it obvious. Didn't they tell you on the unit?"

It was very easy to laugh with her. "I could have missed it in my psychosis. I wasn't exactly with it for most of the time. So what would it involve if I said yes? Do you think I could manage it?"

She gestured airily, "Don't see why not. All you'd have to do is steer us towards a workable design, and help us put it on the wall. It doesn't have to be the Last Supper. I'll take care of jollying the troops along, and all the administrative guff." She paused, "Um, do you mind me asking, are you still on the sick?"

"Yeah." If the authorities believed I was still incapacitated, I wasn't going to turn down their fortnightly payments into my bank account.

"No problem. We can put your pay through as therapeutic earnings. I'll find the forms for us to fill in, it's only two hours a week for twelve weeks, and we can massage the figures so you don't lose out."

"What day did you have in mind?" I asked weakly. "I don't want to miss the Art Project." I sensed that I was being charmingly bulldozed.

"Friday mornings. You come here Monday and Wednesday afternoons, so that fits in. We can arrange transport for you, but if you make your own way in, you'll get expenses, I'll make sure of that."

"I've got a car," I muttered. Not quite trusting my reactions, I rarely drove nowadays. I could borrow Philippa's bike, and claim petrol money anyway.

She was pleading again. "Please, Sarah, pretty please. At least give it a try, and if you truly hate it, you can withdraw and advise me from behind the scenes."

I drained my coffee cup, "All right, all right. I won't make you get on your knees and beg. When does Mission Muriel start?"

She threw out her arms. "Thank you, Lord. I'll be good for the rest of the year. Next Friday."

I caught my cup in mid-air, before it crashed to the floor. "Bloody hell!"

"See, not enough time for you to get anxious about it." She pulled a fat diary bristling with scraps of paper from her bag. "How about you meeting me at Monk's House outpatients this Friday afternoon? I'll show you the wall in the main hospital, and we can have a proper talk. Two o'clock? I've got to rush back there in two minutes for an appointment, or I'd tell you more now. Nice reflexes by the way."

"Gee, thanks. Doesn't look like I've got a choice. Ok, I'll be there." I had nothing to lose, and surely when she realised that I was incapable and way out of my depth, she would find the means to drop me kindly.

"You're a star." She threw the diary back in her bag, and shoved her arm into the sleeve of her dark wool jacket. Her casually friendly tone didn't alter. "It's David Hall's funeral on Friday morning. Eleven at the crematorium. I should imagine the family would be pleased to see you there. Must go, now you can get Bridie to tell you what hell I am to work with. See you, saviour of Mission Muriel." She was out of the door with a wave almost before I could stutter goodbye.

Heather was cynically impressed with my job offer.

"This is how they work. They suck you in with flattery, and soon you'll be wanting us to rate our self-esteem on a scale of one to ten, and do calming breathing exercises before we can have a brew."

"Oh Maggie's not so bad," Bridie said, benevolent with relief at being able to postpone her health and safety report. "She just has to conform with the system, and all its fads and fancies. She doesn't interfere too much here, does she? Now, if I grovel and throw myself at your feet, will you all help me with this health and safety report, and say that we practise fire-drills every month, and have no sharp objects lying around?"

I poked in a jar full of craft knives, which had lost their protective covers, to find an eraser. "Be honest with me. Am I together enough to do this job? Will I be able to work with Maggie? Would it look odd if I went to David Hall's funeral? I don't want his family to think I'm pushy or a ghoul." I couldn't account for my urge to attend this painful event.

"Yes, yes and no." At the shelves, Bridie rifled through boxes of coloured card, "Maggie wouldn't ask you otherwise, and it's the more the merrier at funerals, if you'll pardon the expression. I thought we had some more of that hand-made paper."

"Try the brown box." Heather wheeled herself over to help, and I went back to my Cupid. I had to move forwards, like all the self-help manuals said. I would make it my task this week to drive myself to David's funeral, lay him to rest, and then give my meeting with Maggie my best shot. It would mean that I owed Frances and Philippa a day's work, but I could press on with the wall on Saturday, weather permitting. My Cupid flew down from some added billowy clouds, his grin broader, and his arrow aimed at an unseen heart.

Chapter 4

I ran down all the stairs from the attic, and burst through the kitchen door.

"What about this?" I held up the suit on its hanger for the fashion police to criticise.

"So we dug out the pond like she said, lined and filled it, flung a few aquatics in and I can tell you how many days it was before she got frogs because I went back with some more plants. Five!

Only five days, fucking ace." Young Adam, drinking tea with his bum propped on the Rayburn paused minutely, and snorted at my offering. "Show me the trousers, don't, please God, let them be drainpipes. Frances, this isn't one of your grandad's is it?"

Frances hovered by the door, looking hunted. Young Adam could blether for England, and it was a miracle that he and Philippa ever got any work done. I tried to save her.

"Certainly not. It cost me a bomb." I had bought it a couple of months before I disintegrated entirely, probably in the vain belief that a new classy outfit in which to consult with my agent would shore up my fracturing psyche.

"You were robbed. Still, if it's the best you can come up with, I suppose it'll have to do. Jesus, going to a funeral in jeans, I might have expected Frances to come up with a stunt like that, but I had you down as one step up from her. Your idea of dressing up is a cleaner set of overalls, isn't it. Frances?" She had made good her escape, and he shrugged and re-opened his mouth in my direction.

It was Friday morning, and he was waiting for Philippa to find Mrs Scott-Wilson's shopping list, so that they could make their planned trip to Yorkshire. Pleasurably shocked when I had come into the kitchen to pick up my clean jeans from the airer above the Rayburn, he had ordered me to find some proper mourning clothes. Frances and Philippa had little concept of fashion, and I had become so accustomed to dressing for warmth and practicality, that it hadn't occurred to me that I might be in danger of committing a breach of Millford etiquette by turning up at David Hall's funeral in faded black jeans and a matching sweater. Trusting Adam's superior knowledge of local customs, I had let him boss me into flying up to the attic and ransacking my dusty suitcases.

". . .that gardner Mrs SW had before us was a total tosser. I've never seen lawns in such a state, he must have mowed them with a silage maker, and her borders were shit. . ."

"Sorry, Adam," I cut him off in mid-flow, "I've got to polish my shoes." I threw him a sop and my car keys, "If you wanted to be an angel, you could see if my car will start."

Flattered, he went off, trailing a stream of comments like "see, men have their uses". Knowing that in ten minutes' time, I would be faced with a hugely technical speech about antifreeze, I took advantage of the temporary respite to brew some very strong coffee.

At half past ten, I was clutching the steering wheel, willing myself to drive out of the yard. Philippa and Adam were long gone, Frances was locked away in her workshop, and I was trying to get used to the lightweight feel of smooth fabric and thin leather shoes. I was more confident, I thought, driving in my solid boots. I swore at myself. "Do it. You used to drive down to London at ninety miles an hour, overtaking like a demon. What's the worst that can happen?" I conjured up Bridie's voice, "I came over all unnecessary in the one-way system round Preston. I pulled over, took off the fan belt, and slashed at it with my nail scissors, so I could call the breakdown and get relayed home. A handy tip worth remembering, girls." There, I could transmute any crisis on my journey to the crematorium into an anecdote to rival Bridie's. I released the clutch, and bounced forward over the mud. I arrived on time, with no mishaps except for a car reversing out of a concealed driveway into my path. My foot slammed on the brake without hesitation, and I gave the offending driver the finger, swerving past him with more than a flash of my former elan. Fortified, I sat at the back for the brief service, my mind throwing out fuzzy memories of David.

It was evening, we were back in the smoke room, and he was telling me about his youth, serving his time as an electrician in the shipyard when it was Clough Ramsdens, not Pedersen Engineering, and when practically every young man in Millford was an apprentice.

"Course, it was all Protestant then. You had to be a member of an Orange order to get to be a foreman, and they all wore bowler hats."

I expressed amazement, and he smiled at my ignorance. "Believe me. Mind you, the steelworks was Catholic. When the men stood outside, hoping for a day's work, they had to call out their names, and if you had a Catholic name, you were in with a shout." He shook his head, "Terrible times. There were more men from Millford killed in those works during the war than in the bloody army. Widows cheered when they knocked it down, for all it was a big employer. Not that the yard was much better, was it Bernard?"

Bernard, who had always appeared to me to be irrevocably confused, nodded as well. "No, mate. Mind that time that lad, what was his name, his mother lived by the Britannia, good looking woman, fell down the dock. Sucked under he was, and all they ever found was his boots."

Encouraged, David tried to draw him out further, "You went for being a sailor about the same time I left to try book-keeping, didn't you?"

Bernard's eyes lost their focus. "Did I? I'd best be getting to my cabin. Big day tomorrow. You back on watch?"

David gave him a hand up. Bernard still walked as if he was on deck in a storm. "That's right. Take care, mate."

"And you. Night, Brenda love." He tipped a phantom cap at me, and rolled off.

David's eyes checked his progress. "Shame. He shouldn't be here. They say he was hit by a loose cable. He needs to be in a specialist head injury place."

We both laughed humourlessly. The dead were more likely to rise restored from their graves than for that to happen, and we went back to the TV room to watch the football.

I prayed incoherently that David hadn't suffered, that he had been surprised when the seeping tide had caught him out, and that his heart had stopped beating before he had time to regret all the things he hadn't done. I didn't believe the woman minister's concluding consolations, the tidy exit to a better place, yet I fell in line with the other mourners, and shook David's son's hand at the door. He was tall, like his father, and with the same open face.

"I don't know if you remember me. I'm Sarah, I was with your father in hospital. He was a lovely man. I'm so sorry."

Only the thinnest veneer was holding his grief in place. His mouth formed a word which it couldn't promote into sound and his wife, at his side, stepped in.

"Thank you. Really, thank you for coming. He talked about you, he would have been pleased you were here." Her mouth turned down at the corners. "That's one of the stupid things you say at funerals. Will you come back to the George for the wake?" The old-fashioned word tripped off her tongue without a hint of irony.

"I'm not sure..." I had planned to fill in the time before I met Maggie by sitting in the hospital car park with my sketchbook and a flask of coffee.

"Please." She glanced at her husband and lowered her voice, "I'd like a chat." She returned to her polite inclusiveness, "They're putting on a buffet. In the small function room. You know where the George is? Ramsden Way, before the lights." She turned to the next person in the queue.

Unwilling to appear churlish, a few minutes later I was easing into a parking space in front of the George, one of the more reputable large Victorian pubs on the main road out of Millford. In the gleaming lounge bar, a barman in a spotless white shirt saw my black suit coming in, and pointed to a dark oak door set with heavy etched glass.

"Through here, Madam. We have a bar there, unless I can get you something special." Again, there was no irony in his form of address, or in his sombre courtesy.

I tried to match his manners of a bygone age, "No, thank you so much." God, I sounded like the late Queen Mother, declining the offer of a biscuit, and I attempted to glide through the door as if I was wearing corsets and a hat.

I made the function room, and my heart sank. It was filling up with unknown couples, the women sitting primly behind polished tables, and the men standing in front of the bar. A blue cirrus of cigar smoke was already drifting from above their heads, and their quiet remarks were almost drowned by the rattle of ice into glasses, and the clink of coins changing hands. I contemplated retreat, and there was a touch on my elbow.

"Sarah. Nice to see you here."

It was Alan, one of the more thinking nurses from Monk's House. Relief at seeing a familiar face outweighed my usual jab of awkwardness, and I fell relatively easily into neutral chat.

"You're looking rather smart, if I may say so. Would you like anything from the bar?" He walked me further into the subdued throng.

"I could do with a coffee if they have any." One of the strangest effects of being ill was that I could no longer tolerate alcohol, which was perturbing since it had always been my drug of choice, but at least it meant that I was now a cheap date.

He scanned the room. "My well-developed freeloader senses tell me that there's filter coffee on the buffet. Let's make a start on the pork pies. I know I'm here to pay my respects, though I need some calories before I go back to work."

I had the coffee I craved, and a couple of egg and cress rolls I could have done without, and we talked about Alan's guitar playing, and whether Millford Town had any chance at all of making it back into League football. I saw David's son arrive, his hands held by two grave small boys, and was aware of his wife, capable and pleasant-looking, moving around the tables, receiving condolences, refusing drinks and being a model hostess while simultaneously keeping her eye on them. I was on my second coffee and a cigarette when she finally moved towards me. Alan looked at his watch, conveyed his colleagues' sincere regrets and left, and she fell upon the coffee jug.

"God, I need this. Someone's got to stay sober, and I think it's me. Diana, by the way. I wanted to talk to someone from the hospital." She automatically picked up a handful of crisps. "It's winding me up that everyone thinks David killed himself, when nothing pointed in that direction. What's your take on it?"

I hesitated, and plumped for the truth. "I'm one of the guilty ones. I assumed at first that it was suicide, and was angry at the system for failing him."

She didn't take offence. "I suppose it's natural. But he'd picked up so much this last year, he was quite different from when he went into Monk's House. He'd found a hobby."

"Oh?" I waited.

"Mm. He bought a computer, of all things, and met a young chap who taught him God knows what. If we asked what he was up to, he always said he was working on local history, and looked shifty as hell. What are you doing, Josh?"

The larger of the two boys was constructing a flaky edifice of a layer of ham between two sausage rolls. He didn't blink an eyelid.

"Making a sandwich for Dad. It's his favourite things."

Diana smiled. "That's very thoughtful of you. Don't be too offended if he doesn't eat it all, will you, he's very sad."

"Ok." He slid his creation carefully on to a plate, and wandered off.

Diana watched him, her mouth turned down at the corners again. "I'm not sure if the boys really grasp that they're not going to see their grandad any more. I thought it was better for them to come, though, than be excluded and kept in the dark."

How sensible she was, she didn't seem the type to get an

irrational bee in her bonnet.

"So you think it was an accident?" I prodded.

"Yeah. The only problem he had was his phobia about going anywhere in cars or buses or trains, but he'd managed that for ages. He used his old bike to get around, and if he wanted any heavy shopping, he would meet one of us at the supermarket, and we'd drive it home for him. And he enjoyed walking." She looked away, her eyes blurring, "That's how it happened. His neighbour can't walk her dog so far nowadays, and he'd got into the habit of taking it out on to the beach for her in the evenings. That night, the dog came back and he didn't, so she called the police, and in the morning they...found him."

I handed her the clean tissue I'd had the foresight to put in my jacket pocket.

"Thanks." She blew her nose, "Ah damn, maybe I'll have a drink after all. Then I won't feel so left out when this lot start singing."

I'd noticed the noise level in the room rising as the level of liquid in glasses fell. I shifted my feet.

"I'm not being rude, but I'll have to go in a minute. I've got an appointment at two." That sounded so like my former self, that I was taken aback. "It's about a little job," I expanded, "I'm not trying to get out of the singing. Can I get you a drink before I go?"

She tucked the tissue up her sleeve. "No, you're all right. We've got a tab at the bar." She gave me a shaky grin, "Maybe the traditional way's the best. My husband'll get horribly drunk and have such a dreadful hangover that he won't feel anything for a couple of days." She held out her hand, "Thanks for listening to me."

I took her firm palm in mine, "No, thank you. It's selfish of me at a time like this, but it makes me feel better, knowing that David was happier."

We exchanged further appropriate pleasantries, and I left for the car. I was waiting to accelerate out on to the main road before I realised that I had started the engine, lit a cigarette, and performed a high speed reversing manouevre out of my parking space without thinking about this triple procedure. I shot out into a gap in the traffic, using one hand to find a tape and turn it up loud. Bring on Mission Muriel, Maggie, I was back in business.

My burst of confidence was heightened by the look on Maggie's face when she saw me waiting for her by the glassed in office at the entrance of Monk's House. I had given my name and business to the secretary, who was new, and had taken a stranger's interest in the framed photographs of old Millford on the wall. One bland corridor led off to the outpatients, Maggie's domain, and another, equally inoffensive, to the Acute Inpatients' Unit, where I had spent those weeks in my private hell. It was quiet, with the smell of Friday's invariable fish and chips hanging heavy from the dining room, and only a faint incessant clack of pool balls on the table seeped down from the unit through two sets of fire doors. I imagined the post-lunch torpor, the empty space of time, which, once I had begun to come out of delirious terror, could only be filled with visits to the smoke room and attempts to read or sleep, until the paper man came round with his trolley of sweets, cheaper brands of cigarettes and Millford Gazettes. Like me before him, David had been astounded at the vacuum at the heart of life on the unit. You saw the psychiatrist for a few minutes every week, there was a two-year waiting list for psychotherapy, and the harassed nurses were usually occupied in arcane rituals to do with keeping records and guarding whichever unfortunate soul was in the observation room, or looking after the two or three patients who were really out of it. Everyone else was left to their own devices, and you were lucky if someone on the staff had time to sit down for a chat or a game of Scrabble. We all had our bugbears, from the loss of freedom and dignity caused by being sectioned, through to the grubbiness of the smoke room and the mannerisms of certain members of staff. Not being under section, my particular sticking point was sugar. Either acting on orders from a cheese-paring management, or from their own sub-conscious need for control, the staff allowed only a certain amount of sugar to be put out every day at arbitrary times in the tiny kitchen area, furnished with a kettle, a sink, and two empty cupboards. They were hardly less stingy with the milk, tea and coffee, and I had lost count of the times I had gone for a brew and found that the essential components were missing. Boiling at this ridiculous deprivation, in the end I had forced myself to walk out to a small parade of shops up the road and buy my own supplies, which I hid like a prisoner in a gulag. I still hadn't a clue of the reasoning behind this bizarre war against people already in mental distress, and let it remain as an indication that the sane world was barely more rational than that of the insane. David had always been good for a grumble about these absurdities, and I knew I was ready to leave the unit when I began contemplating bringing in a cafetiere and the best ground coffee Millford could provide.

"Oh my God, I didn't recognise you." Maggie's voice broke through my wandering thoughts, and the heap of files she was carrying started sliding to the floor. "Bugger, help, I must put these in the office, then we can get going."

I steadied the pile, "I went to the funeral. I won't dress like this for painting."

"Beret and a smock?" she mocked gently.

I was so pleased she hadn't asked how I had coped with the funeral, that I took the top half off her stack, and carried them after her into the office.

"Take the piss, and my rates will go up. Where's this wall then?"

"Do you want to see it right now?" She sounded surprised, and showed me where to dump the files.

I rode my wave. "Might as well. Have you got a tape measure?"

"A tape measure?" I might have been asking for a small nuclear device.

I tutted. "So we can measure it. If we've got twelve weeks, we can practise on full-size paper first, before anyone has to touch the wall. It'll give everyone more confidence. You have got a room we can use, haven't you?"

"Don't be sarcastic. We have a fully-equipped craft room, ready, waiting and booked for us. Here it is." She swung open a door, "You've been thinking about this, you dark horse."

"A bit," I admitted, taking in the suspiciously tidy room. "Why don't the patients on the unit get to use this?" I could see paints, paper, clay, two computers and a wood-working bench.

She threw me a look of resignation and suppressed annoyance. "Don't get me started. Red tape, health and safety, staff shortages, incredible blind stupidity. Will a three-foot rule do?" She brandished a metre of shining steel in front of me.

"Looks like it'll have to. Paper and pen?"

"Haven't you got your own? Some artist. Ok, let's make the trek if you're not letting me have a coffee first. I'm sure that college lecturer wouldn't have been so bossy."

"Ah, but working with another lesbian will be wonderful for you."

"I'm beginning to have my doubts."

I started to lose my bearings as we left the unit, and passed through a series of back corridors and doors, including one which needed a security code punching in before it would open.

"I'll give you the code if you want," Maggie puffed by my side. "It's meant to stop patients from the main hospital sneaking into Monk's House smoke room, and people from this end taking a short cut to the canteen for steak and chips. What can I tell you about Mission Muriel?"

"Do you have a theme in mind?" I drew on my mental list of questions.

"Sadly yes. In an ideal world, the outpatients group would decide it all themselves, and we'd end up with an interesting melange, but the cancer staff have requested something restful, vaguely representational, and to do with the seasons. Circle of life, and all that. Nearly there, past this bit."

We halted in front of a stretch of wall.

"Only from the panelled section up," Maggie added.

I took measurements, wrote them down neatly, and stood back.

"What are you thinking?" Maggie demanded after a silent minute.

I amazed myself again. "I'm thinking four blocks. Summer, autumn, winter and spring, with a unifying factor. Perhaps a river running through a changing landscape, or a big tree in the middle, with its foliage altering. There'd be plenty of scope for people to do different things, like leaves, animals, background...I could help with drawing, painting techniques, pulling it together and stuff like that."

She touched my shoulder. "Fantastic. I knew you were the right choice. Can we go to the canteen now?"

I thought we would discuss organisational details over coffee and canteen biscuits, and was unprepared for her carefully disguised third degree.

"One day, I'm going to give the cooks a recipe for vanilla slices," she remarked absently. "Their chocolate sponge and crumbles are good, but they're too set in their ways. You're not local, are you. How did you end up here?"

Before I could help it, I was blurting out more about myself than I had ever intended her to know.

Chapter 5

There was no getting away from the fact that Maggie possessed extremely well-developed listening skills. I forgot to remind myself that this was probably part of her job, as she giggled away at my accounts of how I had misbehaved round the scene in Manchester, before moving up to Millford to wait for the dust to settle from my last reprehensible episode.

"I knew Philippa because I once shared a house with an ex of hers, and she came up here when she inherited the house in Byreby and decided to go rural. She kept telling me how cheap property was, and when things got a bit sticky for me four or five years ago, I followed her, and bought my house in Eastgate." Eastgate was one of the few desirable residential areas of Millford, and home to a tiny enclave of artistic and bookish types, among whom I thought I had settled quite satisfactorily. Before life had intervened so dramatically, however, I'd always had it in the back of my mind that I would one day move permanently back to Manchester.

"So what exactly do you mean by things getting a bit sticky?" Maggie asked, looking pruriently interested.

"I think you may be too sheltered to hear it," I said, enjoying the frustration on her face.

She pushed, banging a teaspoon on the table. "I work in the health service, for God's sake, I'm not sheltered."

I leaned my head forward. "I was sort of seeing two different women on and off, and a friend bet me fifty quid that I couldn't. . . sleep with them both on the same night. Separately, of course," I added quickly, seeing her eyes widen with shock.

"And did you?" she whispered.

I laughed. "I damn well did. The logistics were hell to arrange, but I did it. The snag was," I went further towards her, "they both found out about it, and my name was mud. It didn't even help that I gave the money to charity."

She was nearly crying with laughter, "I'm not sure I believe you, you bad woman. At least it sounds more fun than my sad story."

"And what's that?" I doubted that she would reciprocate, expecting her to brush off any personal probing with a practised change of subject.

She waggled the teaspoon abstractedly. "I was living in York, and applied for the job here because it was a good career move, and what I wanted to do. I thought my partner would come with me, but then she decided not to, and it all fell apart. Typical huh? All I learned was that starting a new job with a broken heart in a place like this is no joke." She frowned then brightened. "Never mind, I found a house share with two wild physiotherapists, so I have some kind of a social life, even if it's mostly with straight people." She put the teaspoon down. "Enough chitchat. We'd better work out a vague plan for how we're going to run the first meeting of the group next Friday."

It was disconcerting how smoothly our planning went, and how well we worked together. Maggie's enthusiasm had somehow survived years of experience, and when I left her at the door of her cramped shared office, I was aware of the trace of an unforeseen feeling which I was unwilling to chase down and examine, lest it should disappear. I would never have dared to admit it openly, but I was actually looking forward to the start of Mission Muriel. I strode to the exit with a spark in my eyes and a definite spring in my step, which was how I almost flattened Bernard and a nurse coming in the opposite direction.

"Way-hay," Bernard rolled backwards into the wall. "In a hurry, shipmate?"

The nurse grabbed one of his arms, and I lunged for the other. Together we kept him upright, and I babbled apologies. I was saddened, although not surprised, to see that he was still here. Too young for a nursing home, too active for a regular hospital ward and too jumbled for care in the community, there was probably nowhere else for him to go.

He wheezed heartily, "No damage done. Well I'll be, it's Brenda isn't it?" I had never begun to try to unravel the crossed pathways which had convinced him that I was a distant relative who happened to be on the same ship as him.

I smiled. "That's right. How're you keeping?" The nurse looked disapproving.

He patted his stomach. "Can't complain. I've eaten worse grub, that's for sure." With the alarming suddenness I had grown to know on the unit, a ray of shrewdness pierced the puzzled cloud in his eyes. "Better than your chum, David, God bless his soul," he said clearly. "He knew too much. They always get rid of the troublemakers."

"What?" I could no more hold on to that shaft of lucidity than I could put a sunbeam in a box.

"The tide was going out. Do they think we wouldn't catch on?" The ray died away, and he turned to the nurse, "Where are we going, Miss?"

Bored with repetition, her voice was mechanical, "To physiotherapy. For your walking frame."

He chuckled, "The things you come out with. Whatever you say, Flossie." He gave me an exaggerated wink, and let her lead him away.

I categorically refused to allocate any mindspace to Bernard's weird accusation. Communicating with him was like trying to tune in a clapped out radio. You twiddled knobs, and received only floods of static, someone shouting in Gaelic and the occasional measured voice intoning, ". . .Lundy and Fastnet, severe gale force ten decreasing eight, visibility poor." All right, so David had taken a kindly, almost paternal, interest in Bernard, and, on reflection, the two of them had spent long hours together in the smoke room, with David reading paragraphs of the Millford Gazette out loud, in wasted efforts, I had thought, to engage the parts of Bernard's brain that might be working. Who knows what secrets of the Millford Borough Treasury Department David had unloaded on him in those strange night time stretches, when the pool table was covered, the lights dimmed and the nurses were trying to stay awake in the office? What if, in the rampaging guilt of depression, David had whispered tales of financial misdoings which lay on his conscience, and they had lodged precariously in Bernard's frazzled cells? I kicked myself in the car park. This was how I had become ill. A crazy notion that the tiles on my roof weren't fixed down properly, which had built up into a towering obsession that had dragged me spiralling down from one delusional thought to another into the terrifying conviction that I was an alien from outer space, not a human being at all. I had no intention of going back there, therefore I had to wipe out what Bernard had said. Besides, there was an easy way to prove that he had been talking rubbish. Nearly every newsagent in town sold copies of the Millford tide tables, and I could stop on my way home, pick one up, and check for myself that on the night he drowned, David had been caught by the notoriously fast-rising tide. Satisfied, I roared out of the hospital car park, and shot towards the parade of shops where I used to buy my supplies.

An hour later, I was in my outhouse, poring over a calendar, the tide tables, and the wrinkled pages of Monday's Millford Gazette which I had retrieved from the basket of kindling and logs by the Rayburn. As far as I knew, the Rayburn had never gone out, but Frances liked to keep fire-lighting equipment handy to deal with this awful eventuality. I double-checked. David's body had been found on Sunday morning, so he must have died the previous night when high tide was at. . .I squinted at the minute print. . . 16.07 precisely. Shit. Diana had said that David walked his neighbour's dog in the evening. Maybe her definition of evening was elastic, especially in January, when four o'clock on a wet day could feel like eight at night.

"What do you think, Curlydog?" I asked.

"I think it's suppertime," she replied from the settee. She was very pleased that I had lit the stove, and changed out of my peculiar clothes into familiar jeans which smelt of her.

"You have to go for a walk first," I said severely.

I bundled her outside for our usual circuit: down the lane for half a mile, through a gate and back home over the fields. My torch made a faint arc of light in the winter dusk, beyond which black shapes massed in the shadows. I generally feared my inner demons much more than physical danger, yet, without Curlydog trotting backwards and forwards, sniffing at clumps of grass and peeing every five minutes, I would have been creeped out. I pulled myself together. This was no way to pursue my career as an artistic consultant. I would forget Bernard's ravings, and devote the weekend to my wall, and to sketching out a few mural designs with which to dazzle Maggie at our next meeting. I raced Curlydog over the last few hundred yards, and let her win, so that she could claim the prize of a square of squashed chocolate from my pocket.

I kept to my resolution, and on Monday afternoon, had a more substantial worry to concern me. Heather didn't appear at the Art Project, and Bridie drew me to one side.

"Claire, her carer, rang in. She's feeling a bit under the weather, she says."

I read between the lines. "Oh dear." Not surprisingly, every now and then Heather went through periods of blackness, when all the good work she did for those around her could not distract her from her wasted body and constant pain, and the limitations imposed on her autonomy. I had only seen her once in this heart-breaking frustration and despair, when any words were inadequate, and all I could do was promise her that if she really wanted out, I would make sure that her second suicide attempt was not as bodged as her first. I didn't have a very high opinion of my ability to cope if she was in this state now, but I pulled out my phone all the same.

"I'll give her a ring. See if she wants me to go round." In keeping with the new, improved me, I had driven into town, instead of catching the bus. Claire answered, which wasn't a good sign.

"'Ullo?"

"It's Sarah. How's Heather? Would she like a visit?"

There was a relieved noise. "Please. I want to nip out, and I'm not leaving her on her own today, whatever she says." She raised her voice, plainly including Heather in the conversation. "How would it look on my CV if you topped yourself, you selfish cow? You know it'll pass, I know it'll pass, we just have to sit it out."

Claire, Heather's lodger and part-time carer, was a farmer's daughter with an admirably prosaic outlook on life, and a penchant for raucous nights out on the Reeperbahn. On weekend mornings, it was probably difficult to tell who was looking after whom, as Heather administered hangover cures and warnings about disease, while Claire lay white-faced on the settee.

"You've no idea what this is like," I could hear Heather raging in the background, and, reassured that she had progressed out of silent apathy, I drove to her house at the double.

Heather lived in a self-contained area on the fringe of Millford, known as the Squares. The houses, built by a mining company for its immigrant workers in the last century, were arranged in three-sided blocks, each enclosing a drying green where washing still fluttered on fine days. She had bought her house here before she started earning what was big money by Millford standards, and liked the slightly raffish neighbourhood so much that she had never bothered to move up the property ladder. This was just as well, given her present circumstances, since her house had a bathroom on the ground floor, tacked on as a modern afterthought behind the kitchen. She slept in what had been the front parlour, and hadn't been upstairs since her accident. One of her favourite threats to Claire was that she was going to wait until she was out, and then call in a couple of burly men to carry her up the staircase so that she could see what kind of mess Claire had made of the two bedrooms. Claire, who was not the tidiest of people, would blanch, and disappear, emerging eventually with a selection of bulging bin bags which she sneakily distributed among their neighbours' rubbish the night before the binmen did their rounds.

On this afternoon, Claire let me in, clapped me on the shoulder, raised her eyebrows and bolted out of the front door.

"Back in an hour or so," she shouted in passing, and shot off to some no doubt gossipy assignation.

I steadied my breathing, and went into the back sitting room, prepared for the worst. Heather looked balefully at me through a fog of cigarette smoke.

"Yeah, yeah. I'm not that bad. You don't have to snog me this time."

I hugged her anyway. "Shucks. And here I was, hoping to get past first base."

She smiled uncertainly, and reached her hand to mine, "I know your sort. Preying on women when they're down."

"That was always the secret of my success." I hugged her tighter, then let go. "Coffee?"

"God, why not. I take it you haven't got anywhere with Ms Warren, if you're hitting on me."

I nearly dropped the kettle in surprise. "You what? You're way out there, smarty-pants lawyer. It would never cross her mind to dally with an ex-patient, and she's not as tenth as sexy as you. I'm still working on challenging your sexuality."

"Challenge all you like. You're more likely to get off with the reigning Miss World than with me."

It was lucky we could joke about this. The last time she was depressed, my attempts to comfort her had finished with an enquiring kiss on her neck, the result of a ridiculous thought that maybe we could work out some form of physical relationship. I liked her and she was attractive, which had been more than enough for me in the past, and I must have harboured some vague theory that we could suit each other quite well. She had rebuffed me kindly.

"I'm straight, you nit. Besides, I can't do much, it would be hopeless."

"Not necessarily." Her neck had been so tempting. "You'd be amazed at what's possible. I really like you."

She had giggled through her desolation. "I'm sorry, you're barking up the wrong tree." A shade had deepened on her face, "Is it going to be hard for you, for us to be friends?"

I had sighed dramatically, "I'll live with it." Then I had been honest. "It was only an idea. I probably couldn't do it now either. And I'm nowhere near stable enough for a relationship. Treat it as a passing whim, brought on by these emotional circumstances."

"Remind me not to get depressed near you again. Put the kettle on, if you're not going to let me take all my pills now."

Her mood had lifted a little, and we had ended up playing poker for loose change as intensely as though we were professional gamblers with our mortgages on the line.

Remembering this, I came back from the kitchen. "Game of cards?"

She was emptying a packet of photographs on to the table. "Well, since you're here, and I have to do something, we could sort out the best of these for Eamon's portfolio."

Together we looked through the images of our installation at the Berkeley Dock. Most of them had come out well, and Heather recovered enough to argue with me over which prints should be enlarged, and placed in the large album which housed our previous efforts.

"What are these?" I asked, picking up a handful of boring views of an industrial estate. Heather's shoulders were beginning to droop again, and I guessed that she wasn't out of the woods yet.

"Huh?" She shook her nearly empty cigarette lighter, "Light, you sod. Oh, location shots. Claire drove me round a few sites before we decided on the dock. They were all too public."

"And too dull." I looked idly at a snapshot of what seemed to be a builders' yard fronted by a small concrete office block. "Eccles

Construction," I read the large sign running below the first floor windows across most of the building. "Where's that...oh, how horrible." I threw the photo down, as if it had bitten me. My skin was crawling, and a shiver wriggled down my spine.

"Fuck, Sarah, what's the matter?" Heather choked on her cigarette, "You look like you've seen a ghost."

I unclenched my fists, "I think I have." I gazed carefully at the picture again. I hadn't been deluded. Coming out of the front door of Eccles Construction was the unmistakeable tall figure of David Hall. His collar was turned up against the cold, and his hands were stuffed deep in the pockets of the lined waterproof jacket I'd seen him wear when he went out of Monk's House to go to the shops.

"Who is it then? Your old grannie?" Heather was diverted rather than apprehensive.

"No." I pointed at David, fixed forever in that unprepossessing place, "You've managed to take a picture of David Hall, the one whose funeral I went to on Friday."

"Bugger me. Are you sure?"

"Totally. When did you take this?"

She thought. "Must have been before Christmas. What a coincidence. I wonder what he was doing there. He wasn't a builder, was he? Where did you say he used to work before he was ill?"

"The Borough Treasury." I sought a logical explanation. "Maybe he was visiting a friend. Or seeing about a new bathroom, or a loft conversion or something."

Heather shook her head. "Eccles don't do little jobs like that. They build whole housing developments, like those nasty new houses off Ramsden Way. No-one knows how they got planning permission...ooh er," she pulled a Twilight Zone face. "This looks fishy. David Hall, loyal local government employee, found dead in suspicious circumstances after a visit to a major building firm. I smell the whiff of corruption and dark doings."

I cut her off, "Heather, don't. I'm trying to keep my sanity around this. I've already had David's daughter telling me that there was no way David killed himself, and someone in Monk's House burbling that he was bumped off. People in Millford kill each other because they're drunk or drugged, and in jealous rages. They don't have the motive or the imagination to nobble someone and make it look like suicide. This isn't the Vatican. I think David drowned by accident, and that's that."

She didn't retreat. "My medical records don't say I'm mad, and I'm prepared to entertain the idea that there's more to this than meets the eye. Who told you he was bumped off?"

She dragged the details of my encounter with Bernard out of me, and we were wrangling over whether Bernard had access to tide tables, or whether knowledge of the tides had seeped into his sailor's veins by osmosis, when there was a cursory knock at the door, and heavy boots in the front passage.

"You in, Heath? 'S me, Whippy. Are you decent?"

"No, I'm naked on the hearth rug with my consultant. Go away."

"Goody, goody." Whippy's tatty body burst into the room. "Can I join in?" He pretended disappointment, "You're a cruel tease. Present for you." He handed Heather a massive spliff, "Get that down your lungs pal, and let your cares float away. Who says I'm not a good neighbour? What are you two gabbing about?"

For all that we called him a drug dealer, Whippy was not a heavy-duty criminal. Officially a handyman, his main sidelines were dope and tobacco, although he was not averse to selling the odd pill or electrical good of dubious origin. He had a romantic view of himself as a latter-day anarchist Robin Hood, and was a great source of entertaining conspiracy theories. I couldn't think of a worse person to involve in a hypothetical murder mystery, and made a series of throat-cutting gestures in Heather's direction. She ignored them.

"You're the man of the moment, Whippy. What do you know about Eccles Construction?"

The little beads threaded at the ends of what had been irregular plaits in his wispy hair jumped in anticipation. "How long have you got? Enough to put Michael Eccles against a wall and shoot him as a filthy capitalist profit-monger. It's his firm, and he's a right bastard." He took the joint back off Heather, lit it, and sucked down enough smoke to fell a horse, "Where do you want me to start?"

Chapter 6

After an hour of deviation and repetition, my head was thick with fumes and more slanderous information on the profit-mongering Michael Eccles than one individual could possibly need. I even had a photograph of this Beelzebub, leering out from a back copy of the Millford Gazette which Whippy had obligingly reeled round to his house to fetch.

"He's always in the paper," Whippy had meandered. "Continually, every day, because he's the chairman of the MDA."

"MDA, don't go away," Heather had sniggered. She was well on the way to becoming very relaxed.

I hadn't touched the joint, but my brain was starting to crinkle at the edges anyway.

"What's the MDA?" I had demanded. No wonder the law left Whippy alone, it would take an inhumanly persistent police officer to extract a coherent statement from him. I had filtered out the dross from his next monologue about corrupt quangos superseding any democracy which had ever existed in this country, which wasn't much since the media was controlled by a secret committee and infant world government, and learned that the MDA was the Millford Development Agency, an unholy partnership between the Borough Council and local business leaders, formed to attract European money and inward investment to Millford. Whippy had hit his stride.

"Their aim is to get rich and turn working people into electronic wage slaves in their cybersystem. That's why they want a call centre here, and why half the college is set up like a call centre already, so they can indoctrinate teenagers into thinking that sitting at a terminal with headphones on is a normal way to earn a living. It's part of a larger plan, controlled from above. Their masters let a bit of ship-building carry on in Millford because it suits the military-industrial complex in the States, and keeps the old-timers happy, but have you thought of why they've developed all these electronic networks? It's not for commercial reasons only, it's because of the control they can establish over populations, so we get used to speaking to faceless operators and not to real people. You know you can't telephone your local railway station or bank these days, you have to speak to someone who could be sitting in Holland or Bangladesh. What's all that about? Making us powerless, that's what, so we only get the information they want us to have, and they've tagged us electronically with credit cards and drivers' licenses and supermarket loyalty schemes. That's only the first step. . ."

I had stopped him before he got on to the microchips "they" were already inserting into hapless patients on operating tables, and every newborn baby. I had the picture. Michael Eccles was the head of a successful construction firm and a prominent figure in Millford's commercial community, and might, or might not, be a minion of the forces of darkness. From all that Whippy had hinted of degraded Freemasonry and twisted rites involving Millford prostitutes who turned up later too traumatised to speak, I hadn't gleaned a single sensible reason why Mr Eccles should have had any inclination to have given David Hall the equivalent of a concrete overcoat. Even the most corrupt local government officials and disgracefully fraudulent executives didn't need to resort to murder to cover their tracks nowadays. They knew that they had plenty of time to salt their gains away in offshore banking accounts and ensure comfortable retirements, even if the finger of suspicion eventually pointed their way.

I fanned the air with the old Millford Gazette. Claire was not going to be pleased with the fug in the house or with Heather's boss-eyed appearance.

"Is Michael Eccles married?" I asked, to forestall a lecture on black helicopters and UFO cover-ups.

"Not half." Whippy carried on playing with the long pincer-like gadget Heather used to pick up objects which were out of her reach. An ashtray fell to the floor. "Damn, this takes quite a bit of skill, doesn't it? He married a Clough. She's from a distant and poor branch of the family, but you'd think she was heiress to the Onassis fortune from the way she carries on." He put on a high-pitched strident voice, "We had such a happy workforce when we owned the shipyards. And when Princess Margaret came to launch HMS Ball-Breaker, every child in Millford was there with a union jack. The Princess told me she'd never felt so proud and humble all at the same time."

"How much gin did they feed her?" Heather made a feeble effort to wheel herself towards the kitchen. "I'm sure I've got some chocolate biscuits somewhere."

"I'll look." I picked up squashed fag ends from the floor, and scuffed ash into the carpet. "How come you know all this Whippy?"

"Any Mars bars? Because I did a little job for them once. Putting up a shed. She sacked me after two hours because I stood on her dahlias. She's sacked every time-served tradesman in Millford, and now they have to get Eccles Construction guys to work on their house. You must know it. It's that horrible modern place outside Byreby towards the coast road. They're always messing around with it."

"Of course." I rooted about in Heather's kitchen cupboards, "The Hacienda. There's some Penguins and Coco-Pops here. Philippa hates that garden. They asked her to do their gardening, and she refused, because she doesn't do shaved lawns and flowers in rows."

All three of us sneered at this loathsome carbuncle in the countryside whenever we passed. The story went that whoever had built it had received planning permission for a bungalow, and had then erected a replica of the kind of Spanish villa favoured by East End villains when they hung up their sawn-off shotguns and lead piping. I seemed to recall jogging out that way one day, and nearly being deafened by an overbearing woman shouting at a pair of sweating workmen who were trying to carry a large crate inside. So that was the Eccles' spread. How handy if I wanted to keep an eye on him. I stamped on that line of thought.

"Anyone for Coco-Pops?"

"Is there any milk?" Heather, gamely attempting to be hospitable, jammed her chair half-way through the kitchen door. "Give us a wee bit push, hen, I seem to be stuckit."

I sorted them out with bowls of cereal, and left them discussing quasars and time travel.

Although Michael Eccles didn't sound like my type of person, I didn't want to read too much into any connection between him and David. As I'd said to Heather, there could have been any number of innocuous reasons for David's visit to his offices. Calling on a friend was the most likely: the turnout at his funeral had demonstrated that he wasn't a social recluse, and it would be far healthier for me to stay rooted in reality, and focus on concrete tasks. I was determined to finish the wall before Spring when the round of work in the vegetable garden started up again, and to prevent my neat piles of waiting stone becoming overgrown with grass and brambles, which would have to be cut away in the autumn. Tuesday was that rare phenomenon, a fine January day, and I forced myself out of bed and down to the garden before nine-thirty, carrying a flask for elevenses so I wouldn't be tempted back to my stove and settee. The low sun held a hint of benign warmth, a robin hopped around me as I worked, and Curlydog played at being frightened by the bantams before settling down on my discarded coat for a snooze. I knew that I went at about a quarter of the speed of a proper waller, yet I fancied that I looked quite the professional, tapping away with the walling hammer, lifting seriously heavy stones without breaking sweat, and not dropping any on my toes. All I needed was an appreciative audience. For some reason, I thought of Maggie stuck in the stuffy confines of the hospital, surrounded by files and urgent Post-It notes, only able to look out at the fresh air and milky sky through double-glazed windows. I wondered if she would be playing football tonight...oh, I wouldn't be there, even if she was. Frances and Philippa were off to an arty film this evening, and Frances had booked a court for Thursday. I'd have to wait until Friday to see her. Alarmed, I stopped bashing away at a stone which didn't want to fit anywhere. Where had that come from? I conjured up my zen thought of a white mountain, and climbed over to the other side of the wall. Maybe this awkward bugger would slot in there.

At lunchtime, Frances wandered into sight, hoiking an old basket. Doris was at her heels, stepping distastefully over the damp grass, her whiskers twitching at anything that moved. She was more inclined to the great outdoors than Ethel, who had probably sent her to report back on Curlydog's whereabouts. Alerted by our voices, Curlydog opened her eyes, and wagged her tail at the sight of a basket which might spell sandwiches and chocolate bars. Doris gave her a pre-emptive hiss and picked her way on to the wall to survey us with a slitty glare, breaking off every now and then to lick fussily at her front paws, or to bully the robin.

"Smart," Frances said, nodding towards the wall. She drew back her leg, and landed it with a powerful kick. Nothing rattled or fell off, and I folded my arms.

"Very nice." She hopped backwards, clutching her foot, "No front wedging?"

"Certainly not. This is high quality workmanship, thank you very much. Want to have a go at it with the hammer?" I held it out, and she smiled.

"That's all right. I've brought a picnic, seeing as it's sunny. And the kettle. I'm sure that old barbeque's down here somewhere."

I fitted a few more stones into place, while she scrabbled around at the back of the bantam pen, and came back with a rusty tray and a crusted water container.

"Forgot to fill the kettle at the house. I'll use the girls' water and replace it after."

If I was ever stranded on a desert island, Frances would be a useful person to have with me. She whipped a bag of charcoal and firelighters from her basket, threw them into the tray, showed them a match, and plonked her blackened kettle on top. I peeked furtively into the sandwiches. Innocuous cheese and squishy hunks of tomato, which was refined for her, since she'd been known to make butties from leftover curry.

"Anything new to report?" she asked as we waited for the kettle to boil.

"Just the mural with Maggie Warren on Friday. I've sketched out some ideas, but I don't know if they'll do. . ." I had decided not to tell Frances and Philippa anything about David and Michael Eccles. I didn't want them worrying that I was going strange again.

She scoffed. "They'll be brilliant. I can see you, thief." Curlydog paused in her subtle belly crawl towards the basket, and gave her a winning grin.

I tossed her a two inch thick crust, and she caught it before it had a chance to hit the ground.

"She can't help it. She had a deprived upbringing, struggling for every mouthful, rejected, roaming wild with a feral pack, before a kindly dog warden with orders to shoot her took pity on her, and took her to the rescue centre. You wouldn't be well-mannered if you'd faced the barrel of a gun." Curlydog's imaginary background was becoming as elaborate as Eamon Bannon's.

"Pshaw. She belonged to some poor yet honest family, who loved her but who couldn't put up with her stealing, especially when she ate all the children's supper. They wept when they handed her over, 'It's her or the kiddies, we can't afford to feed them both.' Ner her her." She laughed uproariously.

I lifted the kettle lid, and saw the rising bubbles. "Very funny, and totally untrue. The water's hot, did you bring some more coffee?"

She blew her nose vigorously, "In the basket." I missed whatever look was on her face. "Turns out I know that Maggie Warren's ex. The one in York."

"No!" I aimed steaming water into the two chipped mugs I'd found at the bottom of her bag of delights. "How come? Did she buy some furniture off you?" Frances wasn't as keen on gossip as Philippa, and hardly ever provided us with snippets of information on her customers.

"Not likely. I've come across her at trade fairs. She makes turned wooden bowls and stuff like that."

"Any good?" Why did I want to hear about the woman who had broken Maggie's heart?

"All right, if you like that kind of thing. She's a bit. . ." she kept me hanging on, "girly."

This epithet, fairly high on Frances' list of insults, was used to describe any person, place or thing she considered fussy or over-manufactured. Herbal teas, fancy restaurant food artfully stacked in towers with minute dribbles of sauce, slippers, most clothes shops and tourist attractions were girly, as was the electrician who had condemned the wiring in her workshop. This could mean that Maggie's ex was guilty of anything from wearing nail-varnish to owning a poodle which had a perm every week, and didn't tell me an awful lot.

"Very attractive, mind." Frances sounded wicked, "Can't think why Maggie didn't hang on to her. Hey ho, back to the grindstone. I'll leave the kettle for you, you should get a couple more brews from it." I knew she had reached her gossip limit, and let her go, stalked by Doris who was obviously satisfied that Curlydog was too well-protected to pounce on today.

I kept on until the sun went down, and a flock of starlings, flung like iron filings against the sky, headed for the trees across the next field. I was pleasantly tired, and my shoulders ached. I would boost up my stove, rest on the settee until Frances and Philippa went out, then take a leisurely bath, raid the refrigerator and snack in front of their television, which, to give them some privacy, I only normally watched when there was something on I really wanted to see. I wasn't sure where this plan went awry. Perhaps it was after my bath, when I popped across to the outhouse to throw my working clothes inside. The sky had remained clear, and a half-moon hung in bare branches at the yard entrance. It was still January, and it wasn't warm, yet the bulb shoots in Philippa's window boxes and the smell of wet earth were reminders that the world had turned, and that winter wouldn't last for ever. Oddly restless, I flicked through the TV guide. There was nothing on that wouldn't rot my brain cells, apart from a depressing documentary on the decline of neighbourliness and a programme about Wagner. I looked at Curlydog, who looked back, and gave me her all four legs off the ground skip. She was full of beans too.

"How about a walk on the shore?" I suggested. She had leapt for the door and into the car before I reconsidered. She was quite fond of being chauffered around, and sat up on the passenger seat, her ears pricked and her nose shivering with excitement, too pleased to criticise me for driving too fast up the bumpy track. This might be her lucky night, when she caught a dozy seagull or a fat rat. It was pure chance, naturally, that the back lane from Byreby to the coast road went past the Hacienda, whose inapt proper name, I remembered from my jog, was Orchard House. I slowed down as I approached, promising myself another supercilious look at its bad taste verandah, pseudo-classical garden urns and glaring security lights. I missed all these treats, because a silver Mercedes swerved out of the drive, and accelerated ahead of me, like an ill-mannered queue jumper who had more important things to do than observe simple courtesy. Curlydog picked herself up from the footwell with a yelp, and I stepped on the gas. Pig. I would catch up with him, and tailgate him to the coast road with my headlights on full beam to annoy him. My petty road rage was vindicated, in my opinion, when I drew close to the powerful red rear lights, and saw the personalised number plate, "EC2", and that the male middle-aged driver was steering with one hand and holding a phone with the other. Double pig. This had to be Michael Eccles, conducting a bloated capitalist business deal while endangering innocent road users with his naff status symbol vehicle. Either that, or he was nipping out for a pizza. I laughed fiendishly at the movement of his head towards his rear-view mirror, and its little jerk backwards when a fortuitous dip in the road made my lights dazzle him even more, and contemplated giving him real grief by overtaking and then hogging the centre of the narrow road at a constant twenty miles an hour. Common sense, and Curlydog's restraining presence, told me that this was childish, and I fell back a fraction.

I wasn't following Mr Eccles either, when we hit the coast road and he turned right, towards the orange glow of Millford. Curlydog was enjoying the ride, and a walk on Trotters Bank would be much more of a fun outing for her than the shore, where she had been several times before. We swept through the dull estates at this end of Millford, and round the curves to the beginnings of the dock system. Gantry lights blazed on the scaffolded superstructure of a ship being fitted out in the wet dock, and the great cranes, which pinned down the land, preventing it from being unrolled and blown away by westerly gales, reared against the sky. I missed the turn off for the bridge to Trotters Bank. Eccles was carrying on, past the superstore and the cinema complex, and on towards the road which led to the new industrial estates. Aha, a crisis at the office. His left side indicator flashed briefly, his brake lights sprang out, and he disappeared. I went on for a few yards, bunged in a U-turn on the empty road, and puttered back to the spot where he had vanished. There it was, a barely perceptible narrow opening, just wide enough to admit his flash car, in the hoarding around Berkeley Dock. It was none of my business what he was doing in this derelict place on a January night, so I went back to the cinema complex car park, slipped into an empty place, and turned to Curlydog.

"Fancy a stroll in a dangerous wasteland teeming with rats?"

Curlydog nearly expired in joyful anticipation. I saw the collar she despised on the back seat.

"Sorry, you'll have to wear this, because we're in an urban environment." She submitted sulkily, and I searched the car again. No lead, typical, she would have to put up with the length of baling twine that had found its way on to the back shelf. "I know, I know," I said sympathetically. "It makes us look like a couple of crusties. I'll let you off when the coast is clear."

Together we made our erratic way across the car park and out along the road until we reached the gap in the hoarding which Heather and I had used last week. Curlydog, who was accustomed to countryside smells, was bemused and then entranced by all the fascinating perfumes on offer. The twine twisted round my legs as she whizzed from side to side, investigating chip papers, coke cans, lamp posts with their myriad calling cards from fellow canines, and, most disgustingly of all, a very old Chinese takeaway, probably dropped on Saturday night.

"You're walking home if you so much as touch that," I pulled at her string, "I'm not having you throwing it back up on my upholstery."

"Spoilsport," her backside signalled, and she scampered ahead of me through the gap. A manky hole by day, Berkeley Dock was not transformed by kindly night. Broken-backed buildings with black wounds where doors and windows had been, split concrete slabs and rusted metal in tortured shapes made it like the set of a particularly gruesome film, the kind in which miss-shapen beings come out after dark to attack innocent dog walkers. Curlydog, who had never stayed awake through a horror flick, was unaffected, and pulled at the twine on her quest to penetrate deep into the heart of this gloriously vermin-infested territory. The clear sky and light from distant street lamps afforded just enough visibility to save me from falling over every few seconds, and I let her guide me to the side of a roofless shed. She gave an "oof" of surprise when I yanked at the string, grabbed her collar, and pulled us both into the shadows. Two cars, one a silver Mercedes, were parked on a flat stretch beyond the shed, and the interior light of the Mercedes revealed two heads bobbing in discussion. A clandestine meeting. I dropped on all fours, and squinted round the wall, considering the feasibility of crawling closer, and earwigging on their conversation. Footsteps, and the click of a cigarette lighter, froze me to the ground. We were not alone. I silently cursed Curlydog who, obviously believing that I was engaged in some weird human hunting pastime, chose that moment to sit down and give herself a good noisy scratch. I tried to seize her leg, and then to stop her leaping up and slavering at my face in her delight at this new game. A cat's cradle of twine grew around her legs and my wrists, rendering me dead meat for any ogre or mugger.

"Wass'e up to then? What did 'e want us for?" A low voice grumbled on the other side of the shed.

I heard an exhalation of smoke, and suffered an intense craving for a drag myself.

"Think that call centre fella's seen his arse over something. He's looking fit to rupture hisself. We're the security, making sure they're not disturbed. Kind of like the 'Godfather'."

"More like fucking Halloween Part Two. They say you're never more than ten feet away from a rat anywhere in the whole bloody country. Must be ten inches here. I could do with a piss, but I'm not getting it out. Might get it bitten off."

"Soft get. You think rats have night vision goggles? Not like it's that big either."

These two fine examples of Millford heavies nearly wet themselves laughing. Under cover of their guffaws, I fought with the twine, and released its stranglehold on my wrists before my hands turned blue and dropped off from lack of blood. So, Michael Eccles was secretly meeting with one of the call centre bosses, whose much trumpeted arrival in Millford must have finally occurred, and this man was seriously annoyed about something. I didn't have the opportunity to discover what had vexed him. Curlydog, realising that her legs weren't hampered by string, decided to lunge into the shed, and then yip with frustration once she'd reached the limits of her makeshift lead.

"Fucking hell." Two pairs of heavy feet scrunched to the end of the shed, and stopped.

"You first."

"Big girl's blouse."

There was no point in trying to hide. I stood up straight, stuck two fingers in my mouth, and whistled the whistle I only used in emergencies. Curlydog cannoned back into my legs, wrapped the twine around them again, and gave an interested bark to the seven foot tall man who loomed round the shed corner, his upraised arm supporting a baseball bat ready to strike.

His hesitation when he saw me gave me a precious second to free my legs. "Fuck, it's a fucking woman. What the fuck are you fucking doing here?"

For all his repetition, he packed an impressive mixture of surprise, alarm and restrained menace into his question.

"Walking my dog." In the minute pause which followed, I abandoned valour. I scooped Curlydog up into my arms, flicked an end of twine out of my way, and ran like hell.

Chapter 7

I broke the Commonwealth record for hurdling over rubble whilst holding a squirming dog. Michael Eccles' hired hand was a big strong man with a baseball bat, but I was an athlete minus a beer belly, in tip top condition from pounding round the lanes in all weathers. Besides, I was shit scared. I also knew where I was going, making a beeline for the gap in the hoarding, whereas my pursuer was wasting energy in swiping at the air with his weapon, and in stumbling detours around obstacles he hadn't seen before. It was still touch and go, until a howl and a crash told me he had tripped on the remains of an iron stanchion I had neatly steeplechased over split seconds before, and, not sparing the time to check if he had picked himself up to continue the hunt, I sprang out on to the pavement, and belted towards the cinema complex. At the sight of a knot of youths bouncing their skateboards around in the road ahead, I reduced speed, and Curlydog's ears stopped the flapping which had ruined my aerodynamics. I risked a glance over my shoulder. No-one was lumbering in my wake, ready to crush my skull with a furious blow, and I slowed further to a speedy walk, finally letting Curlydog slither down me to the ground. She gave a brisk shake, shrugged incomprehendingly at my odd behaviour, and began sniffing out more Chinese takeaways. I felt in my pockets for cigarettes. My hands were trembling, my bowels were turning to water, and mad panic had sent my heart rate off the scale. All I needed now was for these youths to be the kind of vicious thugs who tormented lone women, and I would be knocking at the door of Monk's House, wanting my old bed back. The boys ignored us as we passed, me drawing on a cigarette as if my life depended upon it, and Curlydog straining to snuffle at the long wrinkled cuffs of their baggy trousers, with their smorgasbord of street odours. Another wave of panic swamped me on our approach to my car. Suppose Baseball Bat man had limped to the car park by a short cut unknown to me, and was even now crouched nearby, poised to jump out and batter me? I couldn't rely on my faithful hound to leap for his throat in my defence since, so far as I knew, the only time she had snapped at anyone was at Philippa, who had carelessly sat on her while she was nesting invisibly on an armchair. I pulled my ragged self together. My pursuer didn't know me from Eve, he would have had no idea where I had sprung from, so he couldn't possibly be lurking near my car. If I was really worried, I could hang about the cinema entrance, until Frances and Philippa came out from their film, for which I bet they had been the sole audience, three hours with sub-titles not being most of Millford's cup of tea, and demand an escort home.

The foolishness of this idea struck me after two minutes of hovering at the plate glass doors, glancing in at the absurdly normal world of popcorn, giant-sized cokes and as yet unstained carpet. Violence belonged in the decaying gloom beyond the sturdy metal fence which ringed the car park, not here in this modern enclave of well-known franchises. Taking a firm grip of the twine, I set off for my car, reassured by the sight of two spandex-clad figures pedalling manically on cycle machines in the lighted window of the new gym above the bowling alley. They would notice any mayhem below, and would surely act as a deterrent to anyone bent on pulping me in public. That didn't prevent me from hurling myself and Curlydog into the car, locking us in and gunning out of the car park, another cigarette dangling from my lips. Curlydog sneezed ostentatiously, and looked wistfully out of her window as we departed this paradise of rubbish. After a zig-zag ride through back streets and a thousand looks over my shoulder, I couldn't see that we were being followed, and I made it up to her by relieving her of her collar and string, and stopping at the chip shop on the way out of town. The chatty women behind the counter recognised me from my post-squash visits with Frances, and their everyday flow of comments on the weather, and the sexiness of the star of the detective series they were half-watching on the television in the corner, together with their "just the one bag tonight?" and "lots of salt and vinegar, isn't it?" did more to calm me than a bottle of valium. They didn't notice that I was hot foot from the jaws of death, and so maybe I wasn't. I shared the chips with Curlydog, and thought.

It didn't look good for Michael Eccles. I had no experience of how Millford's barons of commerce conducted business, but I would be mildly shocked if meetings in derelict places with bodyguards in attendance were the norm. Only shady deals could explain why the chairman of the Millford Development Agency had to talk in such a dodgy set up with a representative of the call centre this same Agency was so assiduously courting. It all made a horrible kind of sense. David Hall, late of the Borough Treasury Department, had caught on that Eccles was crooked. He had challenged him, being inadvertently snapped by Heather in the process, and under a month later was found dead. Diana's words came back to me. David had found a new interest, connected with computers, and was going around looking, what had she said, "as shifty as hell". Maybe he had always been suspicious of Eccles, and had confided in poor old Bernard over a year ago, yet had only recently found the inner spark to seek the proof which had led to his death. I wiped my hands on a corner of the chip paper, and automatically handed it over for Curlydog to lick. I felt grubby. I didn't want any of this to have happened, and wished I'd stayed at home. I wanted to be sane, and do clean things like building walls and gardening, without these black thoughts forming inescapable patterns in my head, patterns which were impossible for me to distinguish from the equally convincing unreal convictions of my madness. I hadn't stayed at home, though, and there was nothing I could do to still my disordered mind until tomorrow, when I could have a reality check with Heather.

I didn't find it easy to behave normally when I arrived at the house. I switched on lights in the main house, checked the Rayburn, and sat huddled with Curlydog in an armchair, not watching the news on television, and shrinking at the thought of all those dark rooms upstairs where an intruder could be hiding. The sound of an approaching engine set my heart banging against my ribs. I feared that I was sliding downhill again, into the endless irrational terror from which, this time, there would be no escape, no pills or friends strong enough to haul me out inch by inch, and no chinks of light at the end of its infinite tunnel. Only if the last threads of reason and perception snapped, and I floated off into an amnesiac half-world like Bernard's, would I be saved from sneaking out to the shore, and into the cold Irish Sea. . .

"We're meant to take it as a metaphor, or an allegory," Philippa's voice came from the back door. "The literal story isn't the main thing, it's a vehicle for ideas he introduced in his first film, and is exploring further."

"I still think half an hour of goats bonking was too much," Frances filled the kettle. "Which reminds me. That woman from the farm with the llamas wants to know if we want one. They're all pregnant."

I could tell that Philippa was giving this serious consideration. "How much space do they need? They're quite sweet, aren't they, with their funny little faces. I wonder what their milk's like? Or we could use the wool for something. I've always wanted to be able to spin by the fire. I could make you a sweater."

"Darling, I think they need a field." She bellowed through to me, "Tea, Sarah?"

I forced my dry mouth into a response. "Lovely."

They joined me in the sitting room, and I let Philippa give me a blow by blow account of her allegorical film, while Frances raised sarky eyebrows and pulled faces beside her.

"Ultimately, it's the way he uses a camera, like a painter with a brush, that makes him so special. Hang on, Sarah, are you all right? You look a bit strained. Nothing's wrong, is it?"

Sweat prickled in my eyebrows at Philippa's interrogation. It was so tempting to submit to these waves of fear, dump the whole story on them, and let them take charge again. They could decide if I was delusional, and whether or not I needed to go back to the doctor to increase my prescription for the drugs I had cut down to a bare minimum.

"Er..." Faint shreds of self-respect stoppered my voice.

"Never mind," Frances was unexpectedly kind, "you're bound to be anxious about Friday and the mural. It would be nerve-wracking enough for anyone who hasn't been ill. Come with me on Thursday to the specialist timber place, if you like. We'll stop off at that nice caff."

Doubting that I would make it that far, I accepted her well-intentioned offer, and, trailing a cloud of ill-disguised neurosis, I went off to brave the solitude of my outhouse.

I had my last cigarette of the day in bed, with a night-light flickering in its glass holder beside me. Curlydog, exhausted from the evening's excitement, snored in her box under her favourite blanket. It was so unfair, why did I have to battle constantly with this monster illness? Why couldn't I be normal, and get on with a life, like Frances, Philippa, Maggie and everyone else around me? I wasn't a bad person. I didn't deserve it. Ok, so I'd never been brilliant at relationships, and had probably upset quite a few women in my time, but that was par for the course, and they'd known the score. I'd needed my space and independence, and now my precious self-sufficiency and identity had been destroyed, so that I was dependent like a child again on people who'd managed to stay grown up. At least Heather had a physical reason for not being able to cope on her own... My orgy of self-pity stopped short. I could walk, I could run, I could drive, I could construct a world of mental and physical devices to pull myself out of depression. I'd had a bad scare tonight, but I'd been able to escape on my own two feet, which was far more than was possible for Heather. What kind of friend was I, if I found myself thinking that I was worse off than her, and let myself slide self-indulgently into panic, instead of fighting back, and being there for her? I wasn't starving, or being bombed out of my home, or a victim of ethnic cleansing, or in prison because I was a lesbian. I could lie in my comfortable bed in this peaceful place, supported by the state, safe in the knowledge that Frances and Philippa, who cared for me, were a few yards away. You're a whinge, I said fiercely, quit moaning, and start thinking of seeing Heather tomorrow.

"You let me get stoned," Heather accused in the community centre cafe the next day. "You should've stopped me. I was all over the shop when Claire came back."

"Well, please accept my most sincere apologies. I was under the impression that we were in favour of self-medication." Heather was much improved, and I felt able to risk sarcasm.

"And what are you using today? Caustic soda?" My twitching edginess had not escaped her eagle eye.

"I have my reasons. I had a narrow squeak last night."

I told her everything about my impromptu tailing of Michael Eccles, and my flight from Berkeley Dock.

"I'm worried about myself." I could trust Heather with this, "I think I'm making all sorts of connections between Eccles and David, and fitting in random snippets I've heard or know about David, and it might be real, or it might be my madness coming back. I need you to tell me honestly what you think. Is there something odd about David's death, or were you just amusing yourself on Monday when you said it was fishy?"

Heather didn't let me down. She didn't take the piss or laugh at me, but concentrated, like she did when she was preparing an appeal against the social for one of her neighbours. When she spoke, it was in a crisp, working voice.

"All right. We have the facts. David visited Eccles Construction, and then he died. A long-stay patient in Monk's House said that he had been killed. You were chased by someone working for Eccles. There is absolutely no evidence that these events are linked. Hundreds of people must go in and out of those offices, and by the laws of statistics, some of them will die shortly afterwards. If you were run over by a bus on the way home from here, we couldn't say that everyone who visits the Community Centre will get run over. One is not the direct cause of the other. No-one could rely on the allegations of someone as confused as Bernard. As for last night, you were only chased because you acted as though you were guilty, and ran away. You were trespassing, and Eccles wasn't, because Berkeley Dock now belongs to the Millford Development Agency, and he has every right to be there."

"What?" Her facade was slipping, and she was looking a little smug.

"Yeah. Whippy gave me that gem."

I rolled an empty sugar sachet into a ball, and flicked it dispiritedly across the table.

"So you think I'm one note short of the full octave?"

She stopped her efficient solicitor impression. "Did I say that? The evidence may be circumstantial, my deluded friend, but I don't think you're putting two and two together and making fifty five. Eccles must have been up to something strange if he had men with bats to hand, when he could have a perfectly normal business meeting with the call centre guys whenever he wants." Her mouth lifted up at the corner. "Granted, Whippy and I were pretty far gone on Monday, he talks a load of bollocks, and I was encouraging him. Still, from what you and he have said, I'm inclined to believe that David's death might not have been a simple accident or suicide, and so either I've caught nuttiness off you, or you're as rational as me on this one."

My relief was tempered with a whole new set of fears. Although I wasn't going mad, we were moving into a grey area about which I knew nothing.

"What do we do next, then? How can we find out what happened to David? Won't it be dangerous for us to meddle? Maybe we should go to the police."

She crossed herself. "Hush, what blasphemy. Certainly not, that's no way to proceed. They'd laugh us out of the station, and phone the duty psychiatrist in a trice. Besides, you don't think they like suspicious deaths, do you? They don't mind drunken brawls or the odd crime of passion, but this is too wacky by half. Which is why," she bent towards me, one finger against her nose, "we need to do things the clever way, and get ourselves some protection."

I gawked. "I'm sorry, have we re-located to Sicily without me noticing? What do you mean, protection? Hire our own muscly men with bicycle chains? Shall we draft an ad for the Gazette?"

Heather rolled her eyes, "Now you're being melodramatic. No, we need to have the ear of a Millford bigwig who doesn't like Eccles. And to that end, oh naive one, I have already made moves on my own initiative. I've arranged a meeting for later this afternoon with Ran the Man. You're coming with me."

I must have sounded like one of Philippa's bantams in the process of laying an oversize egg.

"Who? What? Who?"

"Don't tell me you've never heard of him. Ranald MacRanald. He owns half the clubs on the Reeperbahn, and he's as shady as they come. Whippy did a job for him once, and he said that if we need any more dirt on Eccles, he's our main guy. He can't stand him." She jabbed a finger at me, "I was a bit dubious about going to him with only vague suspicions. He might ignore us, as beneath his attention. Now, with your little escapade last night, we've something solid to give him. I bet he'll be interested in what you have to say."

"What I have to say? You're the mouthy lawyer, you can do the talking. I haven't said I'll come with you either."

"You have to. Claire's busy, and I'll need a body to help me in and out of the taxi, and heave my chair up any steps. We're meeting in his office in the Big Top at half past four. I've booked the taxi."

I put my head in my hands. The Big Top was one of the largest and rowdiest bars on the Reeperbahn, and the most frequently cited in the paper as the venue for fights. Claire was a regular patron, and gave us occasional reports on which of her friends had chucked up over the carpet, or provoked a rumpus. Now that I was teetotal, a wild night out for me was going to the village pub when a band was playing, followed by cocoa at midnight, and I had no desire to penetrate the brutal, throbbing melee of Admiral Street, let alone meet with one of the main architects of this hell.

"I don't know if I'm up to this," I whined, "I have to get back to feed my dog."

Heather lost patience. "Jesus, Mary and Joseph. Are you a dyke or a dormouse? Half an hour of your time, that's all I'm asking, half an hour. It might be less if he boots us out for wasting his time. Anyway, you started this, with your banging on about David Hall. I'm only trying to help."

"Help?" She was being very unfair, I was sure it was her who had built up this hoo-ha around David's death.

Her face was implacable. "Yes, help. This is therapy. If Ran the Man takes us seriously, you'll know you're not potty again. If he doesn't, and tells us we're two hysterical women spouting hogwash, it's a warning to you to up your pills, forget all about it, and concentrate on your mural and getting in with Maggie."

I took the easy route, and pounced on her last words. "What's with you and your obsession about me and Maggie? Just because we're both gay, it doesn't mean anything. She's not my type, and what's more, for your information, Frances and Philippa are having a supper party on Saturday night, and have invited a single woman for me. They're in tune with my tastes, so watch this space."

I stood up, and made to wheel her into the Art Project. Philippa had informed me of this soiree earlier today. She and Frances had run across some friends at the cinema, discovered that one couple was accompanied by an unattached guest, and had decided that it was high time I dipped a toe into the gentle waters of being set up with a date.

"She's right up your street," Philippa had enthused. "Young, slim and artistic. She sings in a band, and is a bit of a babe. If you get on with her, you can ask her out for a nice country walk on Sunday. We'll keep out of the way."

I had pooh-poohed her plotting, whilst secretly harbouring a seed of optimism. Perhaps I was ready for a fling, to take me out of this morass of self doubt. It would be something to look forward to, a reward to promise myself if I got through the next few days, and the first mural session, without cracking up. Planning what to wear, and contemplating whether I needed a visit to the hairdresser's, would surely distract me from my real and imagined worries. I would think about that right now, and not about the vexation of this coming meeting with Ran the Man.

I steered Heather along the corridor, "I'll come with you this afternoon if you give me your unbiased opinion. Should I get my hair high-lighted again?"

"You're so vain. Is that house warm enough to wear a top which shows off your beautifully moulded biceps?"

We discussed clothes through the session of making icky Valentine cards, and I hung on to the picture of how alluring I would be on Saturday while I helped Heather into a taxi, folded up her chair, squeezed it into the boot, sat in the back for the short drive to the Big Top, and did the whole procedure in reverse at the other end.

Heather paid the driver, "We'll give you a ring when we're done. I'd prefer you because your boot's big enough for the chair."

"Fine by me, love." He pocketed the cash, "I've a run to the Squares now, then I'll come back anyway."

He swerved off, leaving me feeling vulnerable and queasy on the pavement of Admiral Street. In the glum light of a January afternoon, the Big Top was tawdry, and as unappealing as a pint of beer left overnight to go stale. The neon lights and signs in the windows were switched off, and litter swirled half-heartedly around the shut door.

"Knock," Heather commanded.

I rapped self-consciously on the solid wood. Nothing happened, so I put some effort into it, and clattered the letterbox. One more minute, and we could leave, admitting defeat.

"We open at six." A faint voice came from inside.

I put my mouth to the letterbox. I could smell old alcohol and cheap carpet-cleaner. "We're meant to be meeting Mr MacRanald. Is he here?" Heather owed me for this.

"Who is it?" It was a woman's voice, irritated and hostile.

"Heather Shaw. It's all arranged."

"Fucking first I've heard of it. Wait if you must."

We waited, and I scowled at Heather. "I hope getting out is easier."

She drummed her fingers on her arm rest. "That's probably Vin, the chief bouncer. She's famous. They call her Vin after Van Gogh."

I scowled more. "Do I want to know why?"

Heather smirked. "She cut someone's ear off in a fight. Years ago, of course. She's reformed. Since she came out of prison."

"You cow." I grabbed her chair handles, "We're off."

The door opened, and the owner of the voice was there in front of us. "Sorry about that like. I never got the message. Need a hand?"

Chapter 8

The woman on the threshold didn't look like a streetfighter who glibly severed ears or similar appendages. She looked like any other woman who had seen tough times, and survived on a mixture of wit, alcohol, cigarettes and inner resourcefulness. The hardness of the face under spiky black hair was offset by laughter lines around the mouth, and a cynical intelligence in sharp grey eyes. She was wearing a sweatshirt over faded jeans with bulky trainers, and I couldn't see a Stanley knife making a bulge in any of her pockets.

"They call me Vin," she said, standing aside so that I could wheel Heather into the bar. "Which one of you is Heather?"

We introduced ourselves, and she bolted the door behind us. I couldn't prevent my hand going up to touch an ear, and then dropping it quickly in case she noticed. Deciding that this too was a dead giveaway, I looked around at this den of iniquity. It was big and gloomy, with a huge bar running along most of the wall opposite the door, and a raised area to our left furnished with high circular stools, bolted to the floor and set around equally high tables, just right for falling off when inebriated and doing oneself a lasting injury. A line of booths ran to our right, and I could make out another raised area at the far end, guarded by a high rail, and sporting two shiny poles. Good Lord, they had pole dancers here, how seedy could Ranald MacRanald be? The main concessions to the bar's theme were lengths of striped material creating a false ceiling, together with gaudy cut-outs of prancing ponies fixed to the top of the booths, and I wondered if the barpersons were obliged to wear clown outfits, or swing out on trapezes to pick up empty glasses. Vin led us through a door at the side of the bar.

"Ran's in the office along here. There's just one step down, can you manage?"

"Fine, thanks," I muttered, repressing an instinct to gush. I wouldn't want to make an enemy of this woman. I manoeuvered Heather round crates of alcopops destined for the throats of giddy under-age drinkers, trying to breathe through my mouth without making it obvious, to avoid the pungent mix of disinfectant and spilt lager setting off my gagging reflex. I bumped her down the step, and waited while Vin tapped at a door which boasted a splintered hole, as if some angry punter had taken an axe to it.

Vin saw me looking. "Accident with the dancers' poles," she said straight-faced. "They weigh a ton." She rattled the door handle. "Are you in there, Ran, or have you climbed out the window?"

I gave a polite 'ha ha,' and she smiled guilelessly. "It's been known, although he's getting a bit porky for that kind of carry on. Ah, here he is. It's yer four thirty, Mr President."

The man who had opened the door put one palm over the phone into which he was speaking, and mouthed "Piss off", before resuming his conversation.

"What part of no do you have difficulty in understanding? Am I speaking English here, or have I suddenly switched into Japanese? No, no, no."

I wanted to abandon Heather and run to safety. Perhaps he was refusing mercy to someone who owed him money, and was pressing ahead with a threat to kidnap his debtor's wife and children, and sell them into prostitution. His voice softened.

"You know the deal. You raise the money yourself, and then we can talk more sensibly."

The voice at the other end must have gone into overdrive, and he moved the phone theatrically to an arm's length from his ear, winking cheerfully at us. He was not quite as I expected. Short, early middle-aged with a thickening waist and his remaining hair clipped to a neat number four, he looked more like a prosperous go-getting estate agent than the owner of places of ill-repute. The office was warm, and he was in ironed white shirtsleeves, with the knot of his navy silk tie tugged away from his collar. His dark grey suit trousers bore the mark of expensive tailoring, and I could practically see my reflection in his polished black shoes. He threw up one hand.

"Ok, ok, I'm not promising anything, but I'll speak to her. Tell her to ring me tonight. Still on for the match on Saturday? Yeah, see you there, take care, son."

He clicked the tiny phone shut, and chucked it accurately into a waste paper bin.

"I've three pieces of advice for you. Don't get married, don't have children, and don't get divorced. That was my boy, he wants to go skiing in France with his mates. Skiing, I ask you. In my day we rang doorbells and ran away, and were grateful for the entertainment." He laughed in self mockery, extending his hand to Heather. "The formidable Ms Shaw, scourge of licensees, who put an end to my plan for a late-night venue on Trotters Bank. I'm pleased to meet you at last."

Heather had gone red. "Did I?"

He shook her hand gently, "Remember the Trotters Bank Concerned Residents? You acted for them, didn't you?"

"Shit." Heather's colour had deepened to that of a spectacular sunset. "I'd forgotten. I didn't realise you were behind that."

He smiled directly into her eyes. "Fooled you. Not to worry, all's fair in love and business. Now," he released her hand, pulled up a chair for me, and rubbed his palms together, "what can I get you? Coffee, tea, something a little stronger? I've a rather charming malt we don't serve in the bar. A wee dram, Ms. . .?" He looked at me.

"Uh, Dunne, Sarah. Not for me, I'm driving. I'll have a coffee, though, if it's not too much trouble."

The chair was comfortable, and I was beginning to derive some bizarre enjoyment from the scene, especially when Heather succumbed to the lure of the whisky bottle, and the two of them raised glasses to each other, making twin appreciative noises at the first sip. Vin slipped out, and came back, not with a polystyrene cup of mud, but with a tray, bearing a proper cafetiere, a china mug, cream and brown sugar. The aroma of a fine blend filled the room, and I stretched out my legs. Ranald MacRanald was clearly a man of contradictions. His manner with Vin, whom he dismissed with thanks, was neither distant nor patronising, as if he was the proud owner of an untamed bull terrier, there was no evidence of clunky gold jewellery about his person, and he was charming us with a demonstration of his good taste. I had to remind myself that he owned businesses which did nothing to promote law and order in Millford, and which sucked money and sense from those who could least afford it. He settled himself behind a desk sporting a slim computer, and linked his hands on his stomach.

"I gather you have some questions about Mr Eccles. How can I help?"

I let Heather do the talking. It was the least she could do after dragging me here. She was admirably succinct, however, and managed to convey that we weren't jointly hallucinating madwomen, or nosy parkers bent on meddling in affairs which were none of our business, but two responsible citizens who needed the avuncular advice of an elder statesman. He acted the part well, an expression of polite concern on his round face, until Heather prompted me to describe my visit to Berkely Dock. He put a hand to his brow, shading his eyes, yet could not entirely conceal the suppressed movement of his mouth as I neared the end of my narrative.

He coughed, "Oh dear. That must have been very distressing for you. What an odd way for Eccles to behave." He didn't sound very surprised, and Heather caught his eye.

"Really?"

"Hrrm, brrm." He coughed again, studied the ceiling and then his nails. "I dare say I'm not saying anything out of turn here. If that damn call centre ever gets the go-ahead, the contract to build it will be somewhat lucrative." He shrugged, "It's not unknown for building contractors to apply all sorts of pressures and inducements to win such contracts, so maybe that's what was going on. Not that you should take my word for it, I'm only guessing." He left us in no doubt that he wasn't guessing at all. He swirled his whisky slowly round in his glass, sniffed at it, and took another mouthful.

"Now, your unfortunate friend." He appeared to be thinking deeply. "Eccles built up his business from nothing. He's had lucky breaks, buying crummy land which was then re-designated by the council for development, but there's nothing wrong with that. I find it very hard to believe that he could be involved in something so iffy that it would be worth shoving someone in the briny for, if you'll pardon my flippancy. Anyone will tell you that the two of us don't get on, for reasons I won't bore you with, but I've never had the impression that he would go so far."

I didn't know whether to believe him or not. Heather looked disappointed, and put down her glass.

"So, we've wasted your time. I'm sorry, we'd better. . ." She gestured at me to make ready to leave.

Ran held up his hand. "Did I say that? What you've told me is disturbing, very disturbing." He focussed his attention on Heather, embracing her in a benevolent spotlight. "I wouldn't presume to tell you what to do in this situation. Perhaps, though, I could ask you to leave the entire matter with me for a week or two. I get to meet people from all walks of life, and it's slightly more convenient for me, than for you, to ask the right people the right questions. If your friend's passing on was anything other than an accident, someone will know something and will talk about it eventually. However, it might be more useful for you to remain in the background, as it were. A low profile is often. . .wise."

It might have been a threat, and it might have been intended as reassurance. Leave it to me, little woman, I'll sort out the nasty men and keep you safe. Heather narrowed her eyes at him, and played along.

"That's very generous of you, and a load off our minds, isn't it Sarah? This isn't the kind of thing we want to be caught up in, we only wanted to speak to someone who knows what's what, and who could take it out of our hands. Here's my card, if you need to get in touch. Thank you again."

"On the contrary, thank you. I'm glad to be of service, don't hesitate to call if anything else occurs to you, my door is always open. Let me see you out."

Carried along by a spate of similar nonsense, we processed to the front door, and escaped after a flurry of handshakes.

"Would you mind telling me what went on in there?" I asked as soon as the door had shut behind us. "Have we got our protection or what?"

Heather was bent over with adolescent giggles. "Either that, or he's going to put out a contract on us. What a smooth operator. I think he was intrigued, utterly intrigued, and that we've added some vital interest to his life."

"You've had too much whisky," I said. "What's the number of the taxi company?"

I went on to the Squares with her, then blagged a ride back to my car. It was getting late, and Curlydog would be chewing through the cupboard door. It was a surprise to notice, as I raced along the pitchy-black lanes, that my heart was lighter and my mind steadier. It wasn't that I trusted the unlikely Ranald MacRanald, I wasn't that desperate, it was more the ignoble feeling that we had abdicated responsibility for a can of worms to some other sucker. I decided that if he, for whatever murky and amoral reasons, contacted Heather again only to tell her that there was nothing in our suspicions, then that would be fine by me, and I would put the whole hoopla behind me. Tonight I wanted to organise my ideas for Friday morning, leaving me free to enjoy a trip out with Frances tomorrow, and to making a concerted effort to beat her at squash in the evening, and, apart from the beating her at squash detail, for once it all went as planned. There were no more disturbing intrusions from the cold world outside our snug industry, and on Friday morning, far too early, I rolled up at Monk's House, a stack of sketches on my passenger seat, and an entirely rational nervousness somersaulting in my stomach. I sat in the car, puffing on a cigarette and watching the bleak drizzle seep through a tangled hedgerow across the road. Would anyone notice if I sped off, and phoned in later to say I was ill? There was a vigorous knock on the windscreen. I dropped the cigarette, and almost screamed into Maggie's face, beaming at me from under a Russian hat with the earflaps pulled down.

"Jesus Christ." I opened the door and fell out, "You've made me set myself on fire."

I found the cigarette smouldering on the seat, shoved it back into my mouth, and beat at the upholstery. "If this car is a burnt out shell when I come back, it's all your fault. Don't you know I suffer with my nerves?"

Her smile crinkled at me. "Shock therapy, chuck, it's the latest thing. I'll tell the nurses to watch out for a pillar of smoke. You're early."

"I'm petrified." I bent back into the car for the sketches, "Can I just give you these and run?"

She took a firm grip of my jacket. "Not a chance. I'll make you a reviving coffee, and mark your homework. Come on, procrastination is the thief of time."

Not sure whether her chirpiness was natural or part of her work persona, I let her pull me towards the door. I was feeling more confident already, yet I dragged my feet and complained all the same.

"I'm not a well woman. I have no social skills, I live in a shed and can only communicate with my dog." On anyone else, that hat might have looked over the top. On her, it stood out as a cheerful defiance of the miserable day.

"Then you should get on with this group like a house on fire. Do you really live in a shed? How come you don't smell?"

"I break the ice on an old water trough every morning, and wash my clothes in a river. Only in Mother Nature can I find a measure of sanity."

"You're full of it. Your turbo-charged car is so Mother Nature. Powered by manure, I take it?"

I gave up, and grinned with her. "Nick me some good tranquillisers from the drug store, and I might stay."

In the end, it was so easy, I thought I could make a career as a community artist. The largely silent and wary group which slowly assembled was at least twice as frightened as I was, and fell upon my tree plan with murmurs of relieved approval. Maggie, informal and completely at ease, gave everyone a pristine sketchpad, and produced a pile of illustrated nature books.

"I'm going to copy out of these. I want to do a family of badgers under the tree. Anyone else fancy doing some wildlife?"

After that, ideas began to dribble from the group, first in tentative whispers, and then with something like enthusiasm. All I was required to do was to keep the kettle boiling, encourage smokers to take fag breaks with me outside, and keep saying that I would paint over any blunders.

"Of course you can do just leaves," I smiled at a serious woman with an abstracted air. "You can trace them if you want. I'll help with the colouring in."

The two hours passed in a flash. As if stirred by a magic spoon, people began to chat and make each other drinks, a withdrawn young man produced a series of exquisite free hand drawings of song thrushes from nesting parents to unsteady fledglings, and I discovered that Maggie had not been entirely truthful about the paper supply.

"Admit it," I muttered to her in a corner, "you haven't got any big sheets we can use for a mock-up, have you?"

She was unabashed. "Apparently not. I'll order some right away."

I had a better idea. "I can pick up some for nothing at the paper mill. They always have a stack of free paper they keep for charities and the scouts. I've still got the Art Project's id card for freebies, I'll go there tomorrow."

Revealing a moral streak, she wasn't too keen. "Is that fair? I should go through the proper channels."

I snorted, "And how long will that take? I'm only talking a few sheets, not bales of stuff. They can spare it, it's only offcuts and the ends of orders."

She frowned, "I'll come with you."

"Don't you trust me?"

She looked stubborn. "It's not that. I'm making myself an accomplice, in case anyone finds out and you get blamed."

"I'm touched. What time would suit you?" This is business, I told myself at the perverse flip in my chest, not a bloody date, you idiot.

"Early afternoon? Tell me where this shed of yours is, and I'll come by and pick you up. I'd better give you my number as well, in case there's any problem. Anyway," she looked at her watch, "it's time to finish up here. I've got a free hour, fancy a tripette to the canteen as a reward for our hard work?"

Again, I found myself trying to work her out. Was being nice to me part of her job, or, dangerous thought, did she like hanging out with me? It definitely wasn't a hardship for me to walk with her to the canteen, and beat her to the biggest scone.

"I told you," she said, when we were sitting by a group of medical students, self-conscious with their new stethoscopes, "it was a doddle for you. Easy money, and it'll look good if you ever want another job. Anything planned for this afternoon? You could help me with my files."

I assumed she was joking. "You couldn't afford me. No, I'm

going for a run to calm me down."

She looked out of the window, "It's still raining."

"I'm 'ard, me."

Her hand on the table gave a sudden involuntary movement, and she changed it into a move towards her cup. "Physical exercise isn't my forte. As you may have guessed."

I stopped myself from scrutinising her curvy figure. "You play football. I'd say that was quite energetic."

She began laughing, "Oh, that's not serious. Every year we have a staff five-a-side charity tournament in the hospital. The team I'm in has never gone beyond the first round, but it's coming up, and we want to at least beat the canteen staff. They let me play because I'm not afraid of the fifty fifty tackle, and I'm good at tactics, which actually means I disable the opposition's best players. Do you like football?"

"I used to go sometimes when I lived in Manchester. More for the excitement and atmosphere than because I'm a real fan." A football crowd, with its resident pessimists and stand-up comedians, was a wonderful place for picking up dialogue for my cartoons.

She became more animated. "I love it. I even watch Millford, which is true dedication." She hesitated. "Because I'm a member of the supporters' club, please don't mock, I can get tickets for the semi-final next Saturday. Would you like one? Join me in hurling abuse at the visitors?" She wasn't looking directly at me any more.

I concealed my amazement. She was prepared to be seen socially with me. Was this part of some covert scheme to continue my therapy?

"Semi-final?"

"Don't you hear anything in your rural slum? Millford are in the semi-finals of the Northern Shield."

My face was still blank, and she looked disgusted. "It's the big competition for northern teams in the second and third divisions and the semi-professional leagues. Millford have never got this far, we're playing Wyre Rovers, it's here in Millford at Cavendish Park, and we're going to get stuffed." She elaborated, rightly guessing that I was lost. "Wyre Rovers. They're top of the second division, they've got one of those new breed of managers, Reno plays for them."

I had heard of him. "What, Reno the Beautiful Brazilian? Who scored all those goals in the World Cup yonks ago? Is he still around?"

"The very same. He's finishing his career at Wyre, and he's still a class player. A bit creaky round the joints, but a marvel to watch all the same." Now she was back to grinning straight at me, "Have I sold you a ticket? It'll be in the cheapest stand, and you'll have to put up with me being embarrassing, and shouting a lot."

My radar finally registered that this was not some well-intentioned therapist trying to buck me up, and that she genuinely wanted my company. A soppy glow ran to my cheeks. This was the first time someone who wasn't an old friend or a fellow service user, yet who knew most details of my inglorious medical history, had asked me to come with them to a normal event, and, moreover, had asked me as if I was a proper person, and it wasn't a massive deal. I wasn't going to get emotional.

"You won't throw anything sharp on to the pitch, or get into a fight?"

She shook her head, "I won't throw as much as a sweetie."

"All right. Thanks, I'll dig out my bovver boots and practise chanting."

Chapter 9

I positively skipped out to the car park. This was almost how life should be, doing a job of work, making a funny and companionable new friend, and looking forward to meeting a babe on Saturday night. The sight of two youths on skateboards circling my car didn't immediately dent my optimism. What a killjoy I would be, if I begrudged them their simple pleasures of jumping over kerbs and pretending they were LA gang members. Mind you, their baggy street clothes weren't the best protection against the mean Millford weather, and as I came closer, I noticed the tight faces under damp hoods, and their shivering shoulders. I also noticed that they had stopped moving, and were fixing me with brooding gazes. Maybe they were going to mug me for my old leather jacket. I could suggest that they waited for Maggie and her hat while they were at it. I gave them a brief nod, and fished for my car keys. They came closer, and I sighed. I didn't want to turn into a Gazette "Former Patient in Daylight Hospital Horror" headline, nor, if their intentions were innocent, did I want to engage in a debate about my car's horsepower and optional features. I couldn't think what else they intended, unless they were going to hit me with a sob story to part me from a fiver.

"'Ey," the taller one said, "wanna word."

His voice had barely broken, and on closer inspection, I could see the little spots on his forehead and tears of cold in his eyes. An irritated pity washed through me. The silly fools should be in school or college, where at least they'd be warm, and not flirting with the slippery slope which could plunge them into a hopeless cycle of drink, drugs, prison, lonely deaths in crack dens...

"What about?" I replied brusquely. I wouldn't gain any advantage in revealing my social worker's side yet.

They shuffled around, and looked at each other for support. Oratory clearly didn't come naturally to them.

"Someone wants to see you," Spotty gruffed.

"Who? The traffic warden? Your probation officer?"

They looked baffled.

"'Oo sez we're on probation?" The smaller one tried aggression, and it didn't quite fit.

"Bloody hell." I put my key in the lock, "Spit it out, chaps. I haven't got all day." I was brimming with self-assurance. I was bigger than both of them, and if they were envoys from the evil Eccles, I would eat my boots without sauce.

His companion fought for articulacy. "Dom wants you. That old geezer 'oo popped 'is clogs. You knew 'im, right? Dom did 'is computers. 'E wants a chat."

I successfully bit back a roar of frustration. We had dumped this problem on Ranald MacRanald, and I didn't want any more complications.

"Dom's our mate," the smaller one added, as if this explained everything.

I looked round the car park. There was no sign of anyone else.

"Where's Dom?"

"In 'is 'ouse."

"Where's that?"

"We c'n show you."

"Is it far?" They put on their baffled faces again, and I narrowly stopped myself from hitting their heads together. "I mean," I said slowly and clearly, "can we walk there now, or should I drive?"

"Quicker in the car." Shorty gazed in longingly at its dry interior, and sneezed.

"God." I opened doors. "One of you will have to go in the back. The seatbelt doesn't work. Hold it across you, and pretend." It would serve me right if this was a car-jacking, and they had fooled me with their boyish air of complete incompetence.

The car filled with the smell of wet clothes and teenager.

"Nice wheels," Spotty said. He had installed himself in the front seat, his skateboard between his knees, and was picking through my tapes. I nearly slapped his raw hand. "No CD?"

"What, and keep getting it nicked? You wouldn't like any of those, it's old people's music."

He stared at one of the covers. "Are they lezzas?" He was ready to bully me, and make this ride very unpleasant indeed.

"Yes. So am I, so you don't have to be nervous. I won't molest you. Which way?"

I paid them back by treating them to my best inner-city driving, cutting up other bewildered road users, and jumping on my brakes. On purpose, I missed one of the turn-offs Spotty indicated, so that I could reverse noisily back up to it under the nose of a bus.

I smiled sweetly at my guide. "Women drivers. Don't you just hate them?"

They were both silent, and Shorty had gone rather pale. Under Spotty's malevolent direction, we ended up in a street of small terraced houses which still sold for under twenty thousand pounds (ideal for first-time buyers).

"'S number fifteen," Spotty opened his door. "Fucking lesbo maniac."

"Pizza face," I retaliated smartly, then ruined it by starting to giggle. "Didn't your mums ever tell you not to take lifts from strangers?"

There was a glimmer of recognisable life in Spotty's eyes. "That bus driver nearly cacked 'isself."

"So did I. All right, take me to your leader."

We stopped in front of number fifteen. Spotty lifted his hand to bash at the door, then paused, giving me a sidelong look.

"'Is old man's an alky. Don't say anything." He sounded almost angry, and I cursed myself for not ignoring them in the car park. I could be at home by now, setting off on a run and feeling virtuous, not about to be admitted to God knew what chaos. Spotty thumped the door, and for good measure yelled up to the first floor window.

"Dom, open up man."

The door opened a few inches on its chain, and a pair of eyes blinked out.

"Oh, it's you lads. Hold on." It shut again, and there was a bit of fumbling and rattling, before it swung open fully. "Come in. How're you both doing? Dom's upstairs."

The boys grunted, and started pounding up the staircase in front of us. The man smiled weakly, and gave me a curious little half-bow. He was painfully thin, with a gently face and rheumy eyes, and through the door behind him, I caught a glimpse of a spartan sitting room, furnished mainly with a large television. The racing was on with the sound turned down, and a can of special brew stood on top of the screen. I was pervaded by a desperate sadness.

"I've come to see Dom about...computers." I felt that I should give some explanation for my presence.

He didn't look surprised. "Oh aye. Tell them young 'uns there's Coke and stuff in the kitchen. I'll be having a brew in a while if you want one. Just come through and ask."

Shorty was gesturing at me to follow them, and I put my hand to the thin stair rail, and started to climb. "Thanks."

The carpet had seen better days, but was far less crumby than Frances and Philippa's, and the walls, although bare of ornamentation, had been emulsioned in the not too distant past. From the absence of fripperies, I guessed that this was a masculine household. Another youth was waiting for me on the landing.

"Hi. Ta for coming." He stood to one side, "Make yourself at home."

He was as skinny as his father, and was draped in the same baggy clothes as his friends, yet his gangly frame was charged with an energy lacking in his lumpish companions and the tired shell downstairs. His hair, cut in a style I recognised from news photos of the England football captain, was clean, as were the nails on his bony fingers, and the room I entered was miles from a typical yob's bedroom. There was a bed, now occupied by the lounging blobs of Spotty and Shorty, but most of the space was taken up by two desks, covered in VDU's, modems, printers and other pieces of technology I didn't recognise. I couldn't see any sweaty socks, mouldy crockery, or swathes of dust, and the walls were adorned only with a calendar, a business day planner and some horrifically technical-looking charts. A bookshelf groaned under hefty computer manuals. Two swivel chairs on castors went with the desks, and Dom wheeled one over for me, before sitting in the other, his fingers beating a subdued tattoo against his knees.

"Would've come to fetch you meself, but I was busy. You're Sarah, right?"

"Yes. How did you know? And how did you know I was at the hospital? I'm not being stalked, am I?" It made me very uneasy, to think that these two gormless specimans had found me.

He looked pleased with his own cleverness. "Nah. I was with David one day in town, and he pointed you out. You were with that woman who can't walk. And then I saw you go into the funeral. I didn't go in."

His mouth set, in a way which told me not to ask him why.

"And the hospital?" I prompted.

"Ah well, I was out that way first thing on a job, and I saw your wheels. I asked me mates to watch out for you, and here you are."

"Here I am," I agreed. I decided that it was time to get to the nitty gritty. "It's nice to meet you and all that, but what do you want exactly? Is it to do with David?"

"Sort of." He clicked at a mouse, and suddenly looked younger, "I'm not a thief."

I jumped at this non-sequitur. "I never said you were. I've never met you before."

He waved at the contents of his room. "All this stuff. I work at me uncle's computer shop weekends and such. Some of it I'm mending, some of it was getting chucked out, some of it I've worked for, so don't get the wrong idea."

"Ok," I said cautiously. "Is that how you and David met, through the shop?"

"Yeah. He didn't know his arse from his elbow when he fust came in, frankly speaking, so I started going round to his place, giving him a few tips and the like. There's not a lot I can't do with computers." It came out as a fact, rather than a boast, and his friends nodded, their mouths open with admiration. "I'm going to college after the summer, get me pieces of paper, and then," he made his hand into a jet taking off, "I'll be out of here and making me first million."

Saying "Good for you" would be unbearably condescending, so I contented myself with looking impressed. I still didn't have a clue what he wanted with me, and did some swivelling myself. I didn't fancy spending all afternoon with this whizz-kid, harmless though he might well have been. He left the mouse alone, opened a desk drawer, and began rummaging inside.

"Anyways out, David gave me something, I don't want it, and I thought you could have it."

His hand came out holding a messy pile of papers. He must have taken the dismay on my face for disapproval, and he went into injured innocence.

"It was all me dad's fault. It was all tidy in a proper file, but I was stupid and left it downstairs for ten minutes, and he'd been at it. Took the cover off for something, and nicked some bits for scribbling his bets on. Useless git."

I wasn't going to begin to advise him on how to deal with an alcoholic father, and made a soothing "never mind" noise.

"What was. . .is it?" Besides a pile of tat, I didn't add.

He glanced at it with an attempt to be dismissive. "Some project he was into. About old Millford, or something." He fidgeted, and decided to elaborate. "He made a couple of other copies, I think. One for himself, and another he lent to a pal."

"A pal?"

"That's what he said. That builder guy. He took it round before Christmas."

Oh damn and blast it. My dark thoughts rose in an inexorable tide. I very much doubted that this was an innocuous work of local history, and didn't see why I had to accept the poisoned chalice.

"I'm not being funny here," I lied. "Why do you think I'd want it?"

He shrugged. "It doesn't interest me. Just thought, seeing as you were his friend, you'd like something of his. I could chuck it out. . ." His shoulders had gone tense. There was a moment's silence, then he deflated.

"Look, he told me to keep it safe, and I haven't exactly done that, have I? He never told me the full story either, he could be a canny old bugger." He tapped his nose with his finger, and did a passable imitation of David. "This could be a goldmine, young fella-me-lad, keep it mum." He reverted to his cracked not quite a man's voice. "I don't know what this is. I don't want it any more. He's dead, and he can keep his shitty secrets. But. . ." The confused and frightened boy looked out from behind the entrepreneur who planned escape from his dead end beginnings.

I had a handle on him, and became the trustworthy older female he so conspicuously lacked. "But you don't want to let him down. Well, you haven't. You've picked the right person to give it to. Thank you." I was dimly aware that he was doing to me what Heather and I had done to Ranald MacRanald, washing his hands of a disturbing problem he didn't want to face, in case it interfered with his life-plan. I took the pile of paper and stood up.

"I'll be off. No worries. If it suits you, you never had this file."

I had somehow said the right thing. Dom smiled, revealing a personable seam which would, with any luck, take him far.

"What file? I hope I've helped your computing dilemma. Recommend me to your friends if you're satisfied."

"I will." I snatched at a loose paper which was fluttering to the floor, and scrumpled it up with the others, "Your rates are very competitive, I must say."

He followed me down the stairs, and opened the series of locks on the door, "Cheers, then, bye."

"Drive carefully," a not unfriendly voice exhorted from his room, and I left, pursued by barking laughter. I drove grimly off, the pile of paper bundled into an old carrier bag which had been lying on my back seat. I knew where this heap of typescript was going, and it wasn't on to my unsullied work table, thank you very much.

Heather greeted my unscheduled appearance with exaggerated pleasure.

"You're psychic. I was just going to call you." She had Eamon Bannon's file out, together with a collection of catalogues from trendy London art galleries. "I think it's time Eamon produced some major canvases. Maybe abstracts inspired by his installations. Start thinking about it, and we can go and buy some paints and stuff." She jerked her thumb towards the kitchen, "Get Claire here to clean out the back room upstairs, and you can use it as a studio. She could help with slapping on the colour."

There was a crashing of pots from the kitchen, "I'm not an artist."

"You don't have to be," Heather shouted back. "It'll be just like painting by numbers." She waved at the carrier bag, "What's in yer wee poke? Confidential reports on your muriel group? Are you going to read them out to us?"

She looked different. Her depression of earlier in the week had vanished, and a healthy wicked spark jumped in her eyes. I felt gloomy, and dropped the bag in her lap.

"It's all yours. It's some file of David Hall's. I don't want anything to do with it."

I gave her the barest outline of my abduction and meeting with Dom, and she became grossly enthusiastic.

"This is so intriguing." She began delving into the bag, "Forget Eamon Bannon, this could be dynamite. Aren't you going to stay and go through it with me?"

I heaved a sigh, "Well, I know this is tactless, but I really want to get back for some exercise."

"Aha! You want to be all toned up for tomorrow night, don't you? Don't let me keep you, you're not the only one with a hot Saturday date." A self-satisfied leer came over her features.

"Oh yes?" She was dying to tell me.

"Oh yes. Ran's asked me out. We're going to a concert."

I caught several unwary flies with my mouth. "You what?"

She feigned hurt. "I'm still a woman, aren't I? He's asked me out. The Northern Philharmonia in Preston. Beethoven, Brahms, special place for my wheelchair, supper afterwards, very civilised."

I sat down heavily, "I'm either dreaming or falling into delusion here. What's he playing at? Are you sure it's safe?"

She raised her eyebrows, "You think he's planning to get me on my own, and tip me into a canal? Hardly." She fell silent while Claire crossed the room and disappeared upstairs with an armful of wet clothes. When she resumed, her voice was serious. "Look, Sarah, neither he nor I is stupid. I know he's the closest to a gangster you can get in Millford, and he knows I'm not a weak-brained ninny. We were playing around on Wednesday. But I hardly ever get out at night, and I think I'll enjoy his company, and," she screwed up her face, "I like his attitude. He treats me with respect, and doesn't assume that because I'm like this, I don't have all my buttons sewn on."

I had no counter-arguments. I patted her knee, "Ok. Take some advice from your auntie Sarah, though, and don't let him get fresh on a first date. He might respect you now, but you have to work to keep it."

She hit my hand. "Like you're not going to leap on that young woman the first chance you get. Ring me on Sunday, let me know how you're getting on."

I winked at her, "I might be too busy. Only call me tomorrow night if it's an emergency, and he's got you in a death grip."

I went home, and ran my five-mile circuit. After the first few painful minutes, I began to enjoy the raw physicality of struggling against wind and rain, and pushing my leg muscles to eat up the yards of tarmac so that sweat trickled down my back. Warmed from the inside, I sank into a foamy bath, admiring my sleek body, still the faintest honey colour from last summer's tan. The summons to Dom hadn't set me back. Heather could worry over the file, if she wanted, while I was going to make the most of any opportunity offered by tomorrow's supper party. As soon as I'd used up all the hot water, I was going to give my outhouse a good clean, scrutinise my wardrobe, and remind myself of all the moves which had made me irresistable in the past.

Chapter 10

The old homestead was a hotbed of activity when Maggie arrived on Saturday afternoon. Doris and Ethel, disturbed by hoovering, had skulked off upstairs, Frances was making pastry and trying to ignore Philippa's cooking tips, and I was chopping logs in the yard, kept company by Curlydog, who had been banned from the kitchen and was gnawing pensively on an old trainer. Maggie's car came to rest in the mud just as I was raising the sledgehammer to whack at the splitting diamond I'd tapped into a massive round from an ash which had fallen down in the autumn. I smiled a greeting, took aim, and brought the hammer down with a wrist-crunching blow. The ash fell obligingly into several neat pieces.

Maggie got out of her car. "God. That's impressive, in a terribly butch kind of way. I wouldn't like to cross you."

I threw the logs on my pile, "It's easier than it looks. It doesn't really take much strength, just practice."

"I'll take your word for it. Is this your dog?"

Curlydog, sensing that this was a woman who might have cakes in her pockets, abandoned her trainer, and advanced on Maggie in full "I'm such a lovely dog" mode. Maggie dropped to her knees, and addressed her conversationally.

"I've never seen you at Crufts. Are you a rare breed?"

She looked different too, and it wasn't only the scruffy jeans and haphazard layers of clothing piled on top. Outside Monk's House, she had shed a professional skin, and exuded a relaxed vitality which almost made me fancy that I could warm my hands on her.

"Are you in a rush?" I found myself saying. "How about a coffee before we go?"

Two faces, one with flour up to the hairline, watched us out of the kitchen window as we went into my pristine dwelling.

I wasn't normally such a motormouth, yet I realised later that there had been no awkward pauses in our chatter. Maggie didn't make any toe-curlingly patronising remarks about my outhouse, and she was a hit with Curlydog, who paid her the compliment of bringing out all her toys, and putting them at her feet for her to admire.

"Yes, that's a very nice ball," she said seriously, eyeing the tattered bit of rubber worn to a nasty grey and saliva colour.

"We play tennis with it in the summer," I explained. "On the lawn. Her backhand's better than mine."

She looked at me. "Tell me, how long have you had this problem?"

The trip to the paper factory, not usually a top thing to do on a free afternoon, whizzed by, and when Maggie left, her car filled to the gunwales with the free paper I'd persuaded her to take, I faced an interrogation in the kitchen from Philippa.

"You two seem to get on all right."

I started sweeping the floor, "Mm, well, she's a nice woman."

"I feel mean now. Maybe we should have invited her to stay on for supper."

I nearly scattered my mound of flour and onion skins. "Aw, come on, Philippa, I'm hoping for a result here. It would be like having a chaperone. She's not the kind of woman you sleep with, she's more the kind you can boast about it to afterwards."

Philippa gave me the disapproving frown she used to employ frequently with me in the days before I was mad.

"If you were chocolate, you'd eat yourself. What makes you think we didn't notice you sneaking off to the hairdresser's first thing this morning to get your head re-dyed?"

I leant on my broom, "What makes you think it was only my head I had done?"

She threw the dustpan at me, "Get on with your chores, Cinderella. Those logs need bringing in when you're done here."

The supper party was a success, insofar as the food was good, conversation flowed, and only Frances and I noticed that the cats had been in the pantry and helped themselves to the top layer of cream from the trifle. Ten minutes in, however, and I realised that my drought was not about to end. There was nothing wrong with Joss's appearance: her body was nubile, her dark hair was fashionably cut, she wore the right labels, and her mouth was made for kissing. It was when she opened the same luscious mouth that my hopes came crashing down. Everything that came out was either utterly predictable, or deeply and profoundly boring, and I found it harder and harder to make the effort of being polite. It was galling and frustrating, since she made it clear by gestures and little smiles only for me that she was interested in a fortuitous dalliance, but after I found myself blanking off from her monologue about some new club, so that I could hear what someone else was saying about traditional varieties of runner bean, I knew that I had lost my old ability to ignore personality for the sake of physical pleasure. The brush of her knuckles on my thigh, as she tried to recapture my attention, didn't provoke the tiniest spark.

"My battery's dead," I thought mournfully. "Perhaps it's true that I'll never do it again. My nerve-endings have atrophied, and I've lost my primal urge."

"I hear you have a fantastic hidey-hole out the back," Joss was saying discreetly, "I'd love to see it."

I did some fancy footwork. The thought of her in my sanctuary was too much to bear. "It's not fit for visitors. I'm decorating," I said with bare-faced cheek.

Philippa kicked me under the table, and Frances swallowed trifle wildly. I thought I would put her off further, and pulled Curlydog up to my knee.

"Any treats for my angel?" Noting Joss's disgusted flinch, I let her lick custard off my fingers. It was worth ruining her table manners for the sake of some peace, and I was left alone for the rest of the evening.

"What went wrong?" Philippa asked the next morning over our late breakfast. "You behaved quite badly, you appalling woman. Saying you were tired, and rushing off like that before midnight. Your light was on for hours, I noticed."

Frances made a vulgar noise. "I've never seen you play the reluctant virgin before. It was an education."

I rubbed my eyes. I felt down and discontented. "We didn't click. She was attractive, but just too. . ."

"Young," Philippa suggested cruelly. "You'll have to face it, you're getting to an age where you begin to appreciate substance over looks."

"Bury me now." I knocked back my coffee, "I think I need a long walk with the dog."

That didn't solve my ennui, and I was relieved when Heather phoned me just before it was getting dark.

"Can you come round? We need to talk."

She had her lawyer's hat on, and was making notes on a spiral pad, when I walked into her sitting room. Before her on the table were orderly piles of paper.

"Don't touch those," she bossed, "they're all sorted, and I don't want to have to do them again."

I knew she'd been at David's file, and my heart sank. "How was your date?" I asked, to delay the moment when she would involve me once more in disquieting speculation.

"Mm? Oh, nice. We're thinking of the opera next." She looked smug, "Your gloomy little face tells me yours wasn't a huge success. No luck in the boudoir, I take it."

"It was hopeless. I couldn't stand her." I embroidered the unfortunate Joss's failings, before grasping the nettle.

"Ok, what's all this paperwork, Ms Brain?"

"Odd." She doodled on her pad, "There's several pages missing, including the title page, which isn't very helpful, so I've had to sort of work backwards from the contents to guess what its point is."

"And what do you conclude? Is this the smoking gun, the final piece of the jigsaw which will tell us what happened to David?" If it was, I wasn't sure that I wanted to be in the same room as the gutted contents of the file.

"It's not so clear cut. On the one hand," her arm moved to the left, "it is a work of local history." My heart came out of my boots. "It's all about Berkeley Dock, and there are pages and pages of guff on how the land was bought by Clough Ramsdens, how the dock was built, and the ships that were launched there. Real anorak material, and only of interest to someone who has a sad compulsion to know more than is good for them about dock technology in the early part of the century. On the other hand," her arm moved to the right, "it's more than that. There's a peculiar tone to it, like David was writing a sort of morality tale. I'd like you to read it, tell me what you think." She saw the dismal expression on my face. "Oh, all right, let me give you an example." She checked her pad, and selected a paper from the table. "Here it is, he's talking about the original purchase of land for the dock, and you have to know that this land was owned by a family of fishermen, called the Crossgates." She cleared her throat, and quoted, "According to a report in the Millford Gazette of 12 November 1902, Bartholomew Crossgate was tried in Millford Magistrates Court for depositing a cartload of fish heads and guts on the driveway of Mr Clough's new residence. In his defence, he claimed that Mr Clough's agent had persuaded him to sell his land at a fraction of its real value, by declaring that it was to be used only for storage sheds. His defence was rejected, and he was sentenced to two years hard labour." Heather paused, "God, they were barbaric, and this is only a hundred years ago. Anyway, this is David's editorial slant." She adopted a vicar-like tone, "Thus, the new dock was tainted from its inception by the greed and deception which has been the hallmark of some Millford businessmen involved in this site up to the present day."

She put up a hand to halt any comment I might make about the luckless Bartholomew becoming an Extremely Angrygate. "Bear with me. When David gets to the more recent history of the dock, he goes on and on about how a company called High Tide Holdings bought the dock at a bargain price when Clough Ramsdens sold out to Pedersen Engineering. Pedersen Engineering didn't need it because it was too small, in the wrong place, too old-fashioned et cetera et cetera." She took out sheets from another pile. "This is the interesting bit, keep up please. High Tide Holdings then made a killing, because the MDA was formed, received a massive European grant, and used part of it to buy Berkeley Dock off them for re-development."

"Lucky old High Tide Holdings," I murmured, sensing she wanted a reaction.

"Exactly. And this is the most annoying part." She separated two sheets and brandished them at me, "There's a page missing here. The page before finishes with, "Overleaf, is a list of High Tide Holdings' directors, before the company was wound up. The page after says," she brought it up to her face and read portentously, "Now we can see how Berkely Dock has over the years brought riches to a favoured few, and misery to many. With the worst safety record of any British dock, the crushed bones of its maimed workers must still wait for justice."

"Cor," I said, "I didn't imagine that David would go in for such purple prose." I might not have had years of legal training, but I had grasped the essence here. "Well, I get the implication. Presumably one or more of the High Tide directors is someone whose name the reader would recognise, and be suitably shocked at them making a fortune from the MDA. And we know whose name springs to mind."

Heather looked dubious. "I think that would be a little blatant, even for Eccles. Still, I wouldn't be surprised if there's some connection between him and High Tide Holdings. Perhaps the directors were friends of his, and he was doing them a big favour in return for a kickback. You did mention that Dom said that David had lent a copy of this file to Eccles, didn't you? Why would he do that, unless he was taunting Eccles with what he had found out. He might even have been trying to blackmail Eccles."

I thought reluctantly back to Dom's impersonation of David, and his description of the file as a goldmine. I didn't like to think of David as a blackmailer, yet I couldn't say that I had known him that well after two weeks in the bin, which wasn't your average social setting.

Heather was plotting mischief. "I wish we had that missing page of directors."

"Surely you can find out who they were from your old work, through Company House, or whatever it's called," I attempted.

"Could do, although it'll take time."

"And David kept a copy for himself. We could ask Diana, his daughter-in-law, if she's come across it."

"What, and involve her in all this, while the family's still mourning? There is the third copy."

"No," I said, "nein, niet, non."

On Tuesday morning, I was in my suit in front of Eccles Construction, wrestling Heather's chair out of the boot of my car.

"Don't blether so," she said, waiting for me to click the wheels back on and unfold it. "This is perfectly safe. I'm a solicitor, you're my paralegal and assistant, and we have an appointment. We're tying up loose ends from David Hall's estate. His will mentions a local history work he wrote, and we're trying to locate it for his beneficiaries, in case they want to publish it posthumously as a tribute to his industrious life."

"And you have too much time on your hands, you're bored with helping your neighbours, and you want to outsmart your fancyman by finding out more about David and Eccles than he has been able to do so far."

Heather had sworn blind that she and Ran had not discussed David on Saturday night, beyond a throwaway comment from Ran that nothing had turned up yet.

She smiled ferociously. "Don't forget, I want to rattle Eccles' cage as well. See how he reacts to the direct approach. Nothing can go wrong. The secretaries at work will back me up if he rings to check me out, and I look the part. Never underestimate the power of appropriate clothing and professional self-confidence."

"Or emotional blackmail." I knew that Heather was perfectly capable of booking a taxi with an obliging driver, and waltzing off to this appointment on her own if I had refused to come with her, and my annoying conscience wouldn't allow this to happen. I helped her out of the car, handed over her document case, and brushed fag ash off her long black skirt.

"We must look like a pair of undertakers. Couldn't you find a wig to wear? That would make him tremble before the majesty of the law."

"I wasn't a barrister, you numpty. If you concentrate on pushing, taking notes and being deferential to me, Eccles won't penetrate your disguise. Let me check your nails, I can't have you going in with clods of earth everywhere."

I flashed my hands in front of her. "Would you like to look behind my ears? Let's get this over and done with. This is the last time I help you to meet strange men."

I bumped her over the doorsill, and into the powerhouse that was Eccles Construction. It was an instantly depressing place. The walls were magnolia, the carpet an industrial sludge brown, and it smelled of concrete dust and engine oil. We were in a short corridor, with a glass-fronted hatch marked "Reception" on one wall, flanked by glossy photographs of the worst kind of bland modern housing.

"I'd rather live in a cardboard box," Heather said, a bit too loudly, reaching up to press the bell by the hatch.

"Gewd morning, how can I help yew?" The woman who appeared on the other side of the glass was scary. Trained at the "Every Trace of Individuality Erased!" School of Reception Techniques, from her smile and sing-song voice to the the prissy little bow on her blouse, she was as false as the traditional style fanlights on the doors in the photographs. I bet she wore sterilised latex gloves to empty the bin, and thought that a ladder in her tights was a crisis. She addressed me, but added a "Dear," with an extra beam for Heather's sad disability. The idea that we were collecting for charity obviously hit her.

"Ms Shaw, from Byrne, Williams and Troughton," Heather said with unsmiling curtness. "We have an appointment with Michael Eccles."

She had to look at Heather, yet turned back to me, "Just a moment." The sing-song rise and fall had the annoying intonation of a mobile phone ringing tone, and I wondered if she practised it at night. She returned to the hatch, and gazed at the air between us.

"Thank yew. First floor, second on the right, he's expecting yew."

"Where's the lift?" Heather was good at making it sound as if the receptionist should have included this in her directions.

"Lift?" The unexpected threw her smile off balance.

Heather gave a contemptuous "tcha!", and looked at her watch. "If you've no lift, he'll have to come down. Which room can we use?"

"Um. . ." This wasn't how unfortunates in wheelchairs spoke to the able-bodied.

"Sort it, could you." Heather dismissed her coldly, and decided to be the boss of me next. "If this goes on much longer, you'll have to re-jig my diary, Sarah. Ring the Magistrates Court, and ask the clerk if there's any chance he can put my arson back to this afternoon."

"Yes, Ms Shaw," I said meekly, not sure whether I wanted to applaud her or strangle her with her beautifully arranged silk scarf.

"Where are you going?" she snapped, as I moved back towards the entrance.

"Better signal outside," I muttered, and temporarily escaped my employer from hell.

I stood on the doorstep, and talked rubbish into my switched off phone. Someone was shouting in the yard alongside the office block.

"There's nothing wrong with the fucking timber. If your carpenters can't work with it, we'll find some who can. Now get back to the job, and stop wasting company time."

"Arsehole." There was the sound of wood breaking. "You can stick the job up your back passage, you little wanker. And don't run crying to your daddy when you find that no-one will work for a tosser like you."

The gate to the yard opened, and a muscular middle-aged man, dressed in jeans tucked into leather work boots and a quilted plaid shirt came out. He was shaking and white with rage. I pretended to ignore him, turning my head as if I was involved in some critical conversation, whilst straining to catch what he was saying into his own phone.

"I'm done. . .fuckers. . .several drinks," I caught, and then heard his boots thump off down the road. I also heard the receptionist tip-tapping to the door in her high heels, opening it, and summoning me with a "we poor underdogs must stick together" matiness.

"All sorted now, yew're in the conference room." I had the feeling she was pricing my suit and shoes. "Bit of a tartar, isn't she?"

"She's an inspiration," I said frigidly, and stalked past her to Heather.

The conference room was a grand name for an airless box containing a large table surrounded by plastic chairs. Heather made me park her at the head of the table, so that when Eccles deigned to enter, after keeping us waiting for five more minutes, I could see the flash of surprised anger in his eyes. I felt justified in loathing him on the spot. Short and balding, he would have been nondescript in his beige trousers and checked shirt, if it hadn't been for his quick, almost fussy, gait, and the hard, grating quality to his voice.

"Morning," he spoke fast and impatiently. "What's all this in aid of?" He didn't offer his hand for either of us to shake, and sat down on the edge of a chair.

Heather repeated her solicitor mantra, and pulled a sheaf of papers from her case. "Just a quick enquiry," she said, in a tone which matched his for officiousness. She barked out her prepared spiel, and I studied his face, my pencil poised on a note pad.

He didn't even bother to fake an interest. "Never heard of the man, never heard of this local history. What makes you think I have?"

This was the question I'd been dreading. Heather went for the cold-blooded professional foul.

"You surprise me. It was common knowledge among Mr Hall's associates that he had lent you a copy."

"No." He stood up, "You're making a mistake. . .what?" The door swung open without a knock, and a podgy young man with weaselly eyes flustered in. He looked in a fair old bate.

"There you are, dad. Benson's walked out on us, and now his gang's downed tools."

Eccles looked as if he was going to hit someone, and Heather looked superior.

"An industrial dispute, how recherché. You'll be hearing from us shortly, Mr Eccles. We'll see ourselves out."

Taking my cue, I pushed her past the two men. Eccles hadn't spoken another word, but as I went by, the concealed fury trapped in his body propelled me out of the room like a bomb-blast.

Chapter 11

"Hm," I said, speeding the wheelchair like a chariot to my car, "I don't think this one'll be asking you for a date somehow."

"He might be having an affair with that receptionist."

"Yuck, there goes my breakfast."

"Maybe he shares her with his son."

"You've got a sick mind. She's married, and lets her husband do it once a month after he's had a bath in Dettol."

"With the lights off."

"No, she keeps a bedside lamp on, so she can read a magazine at the same time."

"Isn't that normal? He's vile, isn't he. I'm glad he's having bother with his workforce."

"I think I heard Benson handing in his notice." I told her about the row I'd overheard, and she laughed even more.

"Are you really going to contact him again?" I asked, once we were safely in the car, and shaking the dust of Eccles Construction from our heels.

"I doubt it. I only wanted to check him out, and wind him up. If you ring Diana and ask her if she's found the file, I'll try more official channels from work for a list of High Tide directors."

"You're not ready to let this go, are you?" I looked briefly away from the windscreen to assess the determination in her profile.

Her mouth was firm. "No." Her eyebrows came together, "Look, Sarah, whatever I've said before, I actually find it almost impossible to believe that your David Hall was murdered, by Eccles or anyone else. I've been a solicitor in this town for years, and I've never come across a single case of someone being bumped off to cover up financial naughtiness, it just doesn't happen."

I slammed to a stop at a red light. "Then why are we poking our noses in? Why have you encouraged me to take this seriously? Why all this cultivating Ranald MacRanald, and traipsing around in fancy dress?" My voice was squeaky in disbelief.

She shouted back. "Because I'm a snoop! I want to know things, I want to know who the players are in Millford, and what's going on behind the scenes. My mind's the only thing I've got left now my body's fucked, and I'm going to fill it with as much as I can!"

"What about me?" I yelled back. "My mind can't treat this as a game. If you tell me one thing is real, and then tell me the opposite, I can't cope. It's not funny!"

I revved the engine to drown her giggles.

She blew her nose, "Hen, we've got one good mind and one good body between us. It could be worse. I'll tell you what to think, you do the heavy lifting, and the light's changed."

I made the car bunny-hop forwards. "I'm going to drop you off, and go and build my wall. I know where I am with stones."

She lit a cigarette, "As long as you phone Diana soon, you can re-construct Hadrian's Wall in your back garden for all I care. You're sacked as a paralegal, you're too flaky."

"I'll take you to an industrial tribunal. Claim it's because I'm a lesbian."

"Ha ha. I'll counterclaim that you tried to seduce me, and leak all the gory details to the Gazette."

"I'll take it to the European Court of Human Rights, and have a decision named after me. 'Sarah's Law'. I'll go down in the annals of Equal Rights as a pioneer."

Wrapped up in our fantasy world, we argued all the way to the Squares.

It was Wednesday before I made the call to Diana. That evening, after another defeat at squash, I was nursing my sore muscles, staring at her number in the directory, and bracing myself to lift up the phone, when it rang anyway. Maggie's good-humoured voice pulled me out of my anxious inertia.

"Still want to come to the match on Saturday? I've got the tickets, but I'm afraid they're in the open stand where there's no seating. I'm thinking a hot water bottle under my vest, and three pairs of gloves."

"Should I go to the llama farm, and fetch some fleeces?"

"Is that what they are? I thought those were odd-looking sheep when I came through to yours. . ."

By the time she rang off, I was staggered to see that half an hour had passed, and it was fractionally too late to bother Diana. Goaded by Heather's sotto voce nagging at the Art Project on Wednesday afternoon, however, I snatched Bridie's phone book and flounced out into the corridor. She's a nurse, she's probably at work, I convinced myself, and almost dropped the phone when she answered.

"Yes?" The word was high-pitched with strain.

"Diana? This is Sarah. I spoke to you at the funeral." My intuition kicked in, "Is this a bad time?"

"Oh Sarah, I'm sorry, it is rather. I'm waiting for the police." She hesitated, then couldn't hold back the distressed words. "It's David's house. Someone's broken in, and made a terrible mess. All his things that we haven't sorted yet. His computer's been smashed, his books ripped up, we can't begin to see what's missing. I came home, I couldn't bear to sit there until the police turned up."

My heart stopped for a beat, before drumming in black horror. This was our fault. "I'm so sorry. When did it happen?" A glimmer of hope that it was before we went to see Eccles pointed to a let-out.

"Some time between last night, when my husband checked the house, and just now, when I went round to start sorting his clothes." I heard a door-bell ring. "Oh, I think that's the police now."

The phone was sliding around in the sweat on my palm, "I'll get off. I wasn't ringing about anything important. I hope they find who did this."

A dry normality returned to her voice, "I'm not banking on it. Oh well, these things happen. An empty house always attracts vandals. I'm just resisting the urge to become a hanger and flogger. I've got to go..."

"Yes, you must," I said, and clicked her off the line. My legs were wobbling as I went back into the Art Project.

"Fag break," I commanded Heather, and pulled her unceremoniously away from her pile of cards waiting to be slipped into cellophane packets.

"Oh fuck, what's happened? You're in a doo dah, aren't you?" Rain hammered on the bin shelter roof, and splattered from a broken gutter.

I tried to connect the end of my cigarette to the lighter flame wavering in my hand. "David's house has been trashed. Last night or this morning. It's because we went to Eccles and blabbed about the file, it must be. He probably sent round that goon who chased me." I thought of a baseball bat crashing down on David's computer, and felt nauseous.

"Och, the bastard." I saw the wheels turning in her brain.

"Diana's with the police now. We should go to them, and tell them what we know. I can't stand being responsible for this."

She chewed her thumbnail. "No."

I kicked at a bin. "What do you mean, 'no'? This isn't a. . .a diversion for you any more, other people have been affected. What if they try Diana's house next? She's got children, what if they get hurt? We might get some stick for interfering, and pretending to be David's solicitors, but if it's only your skin you're thinking of. . ."

She wasn't angry at the insult. She put out her arm, and gave me a hug. "Take it easy, girl, we're on the same side. Let me tell you a story. We once had a client here who was arrested for allegedly trying to entice a fourteen year old girl into his car one night. He was a really pleasant chappie, and it turned out that the girl had been knocking back the old cider with her mates, was as pissed as a fart, and had been wandering all over the road. Our client had only pulled over to see if she was all right. The police had taken her at her word, didn't interview any reliable witnesses, and generally made a cock-up of the whole thing. He was released with profuse informal apologies, and bought us a load of champagne."

"So?" I couldn't see the relevance of her anecdote.

"So, months later, he was arrested again, this time near Manchester. He had given a lift to a schoolgirl who had missed her bus on a wet afternoon, raped her, and left her for dead. The police there did a textbook investigation, and nailed him with a stack of DNA evidence, as well as a list of witness statements as long as your arm. I hope he's still in jail."

"And the moral is?" I had been shocked out of my temper spat.

She smiled grimly. "The moral is that if you want to stop someone, you have to get it right. If the Millford police had done their job properly, we wouldn't have been so bloody self-righteous, and a girl's life might not have been ruined. Equally, though, sometimes you have to give people enough rope to hang themselves, and pray that no-one gets seriously damaged in the process."

I flicked my butt out into the rain. "Am I right in thinking you're saying that we should play a waiting game, until we know for sure what was in that file?"

"Yeah. You've seen Eccles, you know he's a lying son of a bitch. He'd probably slap us with a charge, and the police would swallow anything he said." Her cigarette end followed mine. "I've told you, I made mistakes when I was working properly. You make a professional judgement, and sometimes get it wrong, and then it can haunt you." She gave me a look far removed from her usual cynicism. "I've no right to ask you to trust me on this, but that's what I'm doing."

I took her chair handles, "I can see I might live to regret this, but ok. We'll assume that Eccles' vandals found David's file, and that he doesn't know there was a third copy, so we're safe, and there's no reason for him to bust up Diana's house. Let's go in, Bridie's giving us funny looks out of the window. By the way, I didn't tell you, I'm going to the football on Saturday with Maggie."

As I had guessed, this provoked a flurry of "I told you so's" and not so subtle innuendo. To distract her from our flight from the room, Heather drew Bridie into her sadistic fun, and I went home hoarse from denying blossoming romance and fighting off suggestions that the group could make me a particularly sloppy Valentine's card for free.

On Thursday I toiled away through the drizzle on my wall, and on Friday morning timed my arrival at the hospital perfectly. Not so ridiculously early that I looked a complete dork, yet with plenty of time for coffee and planning with Maggie before people started arriving. The beep of my phone broke my assertive stride across the car park.

"Sarah? I've decided not to sack you after all. What time do you finish today?"

"I hope too late for whatever you're planning." Today I wanted to be a community artist, not a gangster's moll's gopher.

"I'm guessing it's around midday. Am I right?"

"Sadly, yes."

"Don't get het up, everything's cool. Can you pop round, pick me up, and come with me to the Big Top? A working lunch with Ran."

I squawked into the phone.

"He's paying. And if you don't come, you won't get to hear my interesting news."

"Tell me over the phone, you Tartan trollop."

"Racist. See you later."

The phone went dead, and I ground my teeth. It had only taken a week for Mission Muriel to turn from a possible cause of another breakdown into an additional foothold in the world of sanity, and I was damned if Heather was going to bugger up this morning's session for me. I did some breathing exercises, thought of trees and went inside.

"Darn, Sarah, I can't get these to look like badgers."

There were a few covert artists in the group, and Maggie, to be honest, was not one of them. I examined the sketchbook she shoved across to me, and tried to hide my smile.

"I think your main problem is with their heads." They looked more like zebras. "I know they're smaller than we want in the book, but why don't you trace them, so you get a feeling for their shape, and then try them bigger freehand afterwards."

"That's cheating." She took the sketchbook back, rubbed out a few lines, and picked up her pencil again. Low level chat surrounded us.

"Could you pass the rubber, please?"

"Do foxes hibernate?"

"I was in for three months, Christmas and all."

"I wouldn't let them put me there. I pulled out the tubes and legged it before the psychiatrist came."

The tiny frown had returned to the top of Maggie's nose, and her hand, gripping the pencil, was small and pink. She drew another line, her eyes almost crossed in concentration. My teeth clamped down on the crayon in my mouth as a bubble of sweet and intense desire swelled and burst in my chest. I wanted to tuck that curl behind her ear, run my finger along her jaw, tilt those lips up to mine, and. . ."

"Sarah, will we be able to practise with paints on paper before we go on the wall?"

My cheeks burning, I turned to my questioner. "Oh yes, yes,

indeed, of course," I babbled. "Lots of practice, as much as you want. . .I'm putting the kettle on."

"Good idea," Maggie threw down her pencil, "I'll help you. Who wants what?" Her voice was music dancing along my breastbone.

"Don't let her look at me," I prayed, rushing to the kettle. "Don't let her know what I'm thinking."

She stood close to me, turning mugs from the draining board up the right way, and subjecting them to quality control.

"Clean, clean, passable, inevitable food poisoning." She dropped one back into the sink. "Is that kettle switched on at the wall?"

"Yes. . .I mean no." I pressed the switch.

"It helps." She turned round, and leant against the sink and cupboard unit, her arms folded over the generous rise of her breasts. How wonderful it would be to slip one arm around her waist, and let my other hand move slowly down from her shoulder, watching her hazel eyes dissolve into pleasure, and feeling her respond against my palm. A flutter, fortunately invisible, told me my battery was far from dead. Oh hell, this was appalling, they must be able to hear my heart pounding from the other side of the room, and I had to say something, anything, to drown its echoing boom. My mind was a total blank.

"How's your canine familiar?" Maggie sounded no different, although how she could be unaware that I was a bundle of untimely lust I had no idea.

"In disgrace." Praise the lord, recognisable words were coming from my mouth. "She ate Philippa's snowdrops yesterday. She forgot from last year that they weren't sweets and didn't taste nice. She might have got away with it, if she hadn't come inside and spat a mouthful of stems out on to the kitchen floor." It was now my life's ambition to make her laugh like this for ever, and I cursed Heather's stupid arrangement with Ran, which would take me away from the miracle of her presence at twelve o'clock, and scupper any chances of sitting with her in the canteen, wallowing in these new feelings.

The rest of the morning passed in a tingling teenage blur of attempting to be cool, whilst dying with happiness inside every time Maggie spoke to me or smiled in my direction.

"Still up for tomorrow?" She stood with me in the doorway as I was about to leave.

I made my eyes meet hers, and tried not to kid myself that there was anything more than friendliness in their entrancing depths.

"Of course. I've looked out my thermals and knuckledusters."

"Terrific. I'll come by at around twelve thirty. Is that too early?"

"Not at all. See you then."

"Looking forward to it. See you, chuck."

More bubbles fizzled and popped. I would willingly stand on hot coals watching paint dry if she was there beside me, with her tilty nose and ripe body promising hours of lingering delight. . . I gave myself a series of severe verbal warnings on the drive to Heather's. She was a professional, I had been a patient, there was categorically no way she would fool around with me, even if she wanted to, which she probably didn't, because she would never arrange to spend time with me if there was any danger of her being tempted to break the occupational therapists' code of ethics, which most likely had not going to bed with your clients as number one on the list. Aha, a rebellious voice whispered, she calls me chuck, she had said she was looking forward to tomorrow, she had almost touched me when we said goodbye. Don't go there, I warned the tender green shoots of awakening nerves, do you really want to have to tell Heather that she was right about you and her? That shut me up, and I arrived at Heather's with everything well under control.

"You look different," she remarked, defying me to help her with her seat belt. "Sort of glowy and smiley."

"It's the prospect of having lunch with you, my dear," I said in my best seductress voice. "Ran is clearly my rival for your affections, so when you see us both together, you'll realise how I outshine him in all departments."

"Except the hairy chest one." She knocked her document case to the floor, and I didn't pick it up for her.

"How do you know he's got a hairy chest? He didn't take his shirt off in the Brahms, did he, the oaf?"

She struggled to reach the case. "He's bound to have one, isn't he. Men who are going bald like that are usually well-endowed in other areas."

"Bleah. I might have a hairy chest for all you know."

"Not the right texture, and your bumps are the wrong shape. Are you going to start this car, or are we sitting here for show?" She had retrieved her case, and I pulled the keys from the ignition.

"Not until you tell me your news. I want to hear it before Ran."

"You're a hard besom." She unzipped the case, "This isn't me submitting to threats, it's me being kind to someone who hasn't a chance with me. Have a look at this, hen, it's your smoking gun. They couriered it round from my old office this morning."

I took the piece of shiny fax paper, and deciphered the smudged black print. It was a message from a firm of city solicitors about an office block, and I jumped to the end where a postscript added, "Here is the other information you requested. The directors of High Tide Holdings were:" There followed a list of names I didn't recognise, apart from one, which Heather had highlighted with magic marker.

"E Clough?" I raised my eyebrows at her. "One of the shipyard Cloughs?"

She smiled, "More than that. I consulted Whippy. We went through Edwards, Ethelreds and Engleberts until it hit us that we were sexist bigots. It's Evadne, Evadne Clough, the loyal and beloved spouse of. . ."

"Michael Eccles." I started the engine, "Now we've got him, the money-grubbing toe-rag."

Chapter 12

Our reception at the Big Top was somewhat different from our first visit. The door opened before I had a chance to knock, and Vin was there, the sharpness of her eyes mellowed into what seemed like a natural warmth.

"All right? Here, let me." She took Heather's chair and spoke quickly to her, "Please be kind to Ran. He decided to order in stuff for lunch, so make out that it's all delicious." She coloured slightly, "It's not that he doesn't want to be seen out with you, love, he's just paranoid about eating in Millford. He has delusions of whatsit, thinks that all the chefs will spit into his soup or worse. It all started when he got ill from a dodgy Chinese." She glanced at me, and the sharpness had returned, "You're an artist, I hear. What d'you think of the new sculpture on the roundabout?"

I hummed and hawed. This bold and evocative representation of Millford's industrial past, a tangled mash of steel girders, was either a cause for civic pride or a complete waste of hard cash, depending on your point of view. I cautioned myself not to assume that Vin was a philistine, she might be a connoisseur of monumental art, I mustn't speak down to her.

"The Scrap in the Bap? It's not to my taste. Too derivative, and I think they could have got something more exciting for the money."

"Like what?" She was looking at me quite acutely now. Maybe she was measuring up my ears.

I shrugged. "I don't know. Something like a ship coming out of the roundabout, or a submarine, or a bunch of riveters."

She negotiated the step down towards the office. "I see what you mean. I still like it better than a poncy old git on a plinth, though, which is what we could have got. There's quite a bit of skill gone into welding it like that."

"And she should know." Ran was standing at his office door, "She's a dab hand with the welding iron. Come away in, the food's ready."

Today, his shirt had a charcoal stripe, and his tie was a deep maroon, and I was startled by the way he stepped forward and kissed Heather's cheek, as if this was a familiar gesture between them. Joking was one thing, but surely there couldn't be anything serious going on? He wasn't respectable, and Heather was a... A what? I caught my thoughts, and was furious with myself. Did I mean a lawyer, or a cripple? I was a disgusting hypocrite, and no better than that dreadful receptionist. Here I was, a person with a history of psychiatric disorder, fantasising over an unsuspecting therapist who treated me decently, and still daring to cast judgement on my friend. They were both adults, and could do as they pleased.

"Coffee for you again?" Vin's voice in my ear prevented me from catching what Heather was murmuring to Ran.

"Yeah. I mean," I turned to her, "thanks. I'll do it, if you show me where the things are."

"Ok." She drew me back into the passage, "Give them a minute to catch up, I suppose."

I followed her to a cubby-hole of a kitchen, and instantly felt redundant as she flipped efficiently around the cupboards.

She indicated the top of a unit, "There's a tray up there. It might need a wipe."

Glad of something to do, I reached the tray down, and took it to the small sink.

"The advantage of being tall," she said amiably.

I was getting fed up with my inability to come up with safe topics of conversation that day. Asking her how long she had worked for Ran might be too prying, and discussing which blend of coffee she was spooning into the cafetiere would be simply inane. Go for it, I sneered internally, ask her how long she was inside, it's what you're dying to know. Gusts of laughter came from the office, and we looked at each other. Her eyes sized me up.

"You're good mates with Heather." It fell somewhere between a statement and a question.

"Yes." That came out like a challenge.

She bobbed her head. "You don't have to take my word for it, but Ran's not a bastard with women."

I stopped my obsessive tray wiping. "I'm relieved to hear it." I hadn't intended to sound so dry.

"I bet." Her gaze, if not hostile, was uncomfortably penetrating. "Fancy her yourself?"

Now I was fed up with trying not to provoke her, and with the overcharged atmosphere in this tiny space.

"What kind of sad sack do you think I am? I don't need to waste my energy on straights. I'm her friend, full stop." That's torn it, I thought, she'll open a drawer, pull out a big knife, and it'll be goodbye to one or more of my attractive features.

She put up a hand, "Whoa, point taken. Just trying to figure you out, that's all. I'm paid to watch Ranald's back, I don't need some big hard dyke with a grudge against him lurking in the shadows."

I had never heard anything so absurd or unexpected. I was a spineless wreck, that much should be obvious to anyone, let alone to an ex-con.

"I'm not a big hard dyke."

"No? You give a good imitation of one."

I couldn't stop the flattered laugh escaping through my nostrils.

"Really? How? Is it my boots?"

She grinned back at me, "And the ring in your eyebrow, and the way you walk, and your snotty expression. How many tattoos have you got?"

"Just the one. I didn't know I looked snotty, I thought I looked nervous."

She gave me another perceptive look. "I can see it now. You haven't been inside, have you?"

I felt inadequate. "No. Only the bin."

She seemed satisfied, "Same difference, probably."

Awkwardly, I touched the counter, near to where her hand lay. "I don't want Heather to get hurt. But I'm not jealous, and I'm certainly not a lurker."

Smiling again, she poured boiling water into the coffee pot. "I'm glad we've got that cleared up. As I said, Ran's not a bastard around the ladies. He'd probably like to be, mind, but he can't quite pull it off. He let his wife take him to the cleaners, and he's usually the one who gets dumped. So if your friend's got anything about her, which I think she has, she should be all right." Her mouth stiffened, "Don't get me wrong. Ran's not St Francis of Fucking Assissi, extending a helping hand to those who've had a raw deal. Yeah, he gave me a chance, but he employs me because my reputation is an advantage for him. He'll be getting something from Heather, even if it's only the company of a woman whose IQ is above the single figure range of most of his punters."

"He has you around. You're not stupid." If I came across as fearless, I might as well act on it, and live to regret it later.

She picked up the tray. "I'm not educated like she is. Besides, I like my men a little rougher round the edges."

"I see." I suppose that made sense, with her history.

"Do you?" She put the tray down again, "Since we're speaking plainly, I'll let you into a secret. I never cut anyone's ear off. A nasty cut, yes, but a full amputation, no. I was younger, angrier and ten times dumber than I am now. Still, it makes my job a lot easier if people believe I did, and I like my job. I'm not cut out for the nine to five, and I don't see myself being sweet to old ladies in a nursing home, even if I could get a job in one with my record, which I couldn't. Oh fuck it," she jeered at herself, "what I'm trying to say is that you don't have to be scared of me, but don't you dare pity me. I can make the most of what I've got."

I took the tray from the surface. "That's a relief. I'll stop worrying about whether I'm going to leave here with both ears in place."

"Cheeky cow." She made a cutting motion with her fingers towards my head, and we walked amicably back to the office.

Ran had made an effort with the lunch. On his cleared desk, I saw sophisticated canapés, smoked salmon sandwiches, bowls of olives drenched in herby olive oil and miniature danish pastries among the various treats, and he and Heather were glugging back a chilled white wine. At a quick signal from Ran, Vin stayed in the room, shutting the door behind her, and moving to the desk,

"Can we start eating the profits now?"

Smoked salmon was a rare luxury for me, and I took a handful of sandwiches. Although they didn't quite make up for being wrenched from Maggie, it was high quality stuff which melted in my mouth, and I sneaked a couple into my pocket, to give to Curlydog later on. After a few minutes of polite chewing and well-bred conversation about the weather, Ran spat an olive pit into his palm.

"I suppose we'd better talk business to make this tax deductible. What's the latest?"

Heather produced the fax, "I have in my hand a piece of paper. . ."

Ran and Vin sat immobile, jaws stuck, while she gave a dramatised account of the past week.

"The file's in my case," she finished. "You can borrow it if you like."

Ran took the fax, his face a picture. No longer the suave charmer, I guessed that he was struggling with disbelief that Heather had discovered something which he didn't know.

"Arse," he said finally. "That fucker. I knew he was pulling a fast one over that dock." Absently, he put a whole pastry into his mouth, his eyes boring through the office walls, probably to a vista of Eccles bound to a chair being tortured with secateurs in an unused warehouse. The taste of ruthlessness tainted the smoked salmon on my tongue. I looked at Vin. The lines round her mouth were twitching and deepening, and her spiky hair was beginning to shake.

"It's more creative than mugging." She released a peal of laughter, and I feared for her life.

Ran's giggle was infectious. "You have to give it to him. He hasn't an ounce of shame. Still, neither have I. Happiness is the best revenge, they say, and what I've got planned for him is going to make me very happy indeed." He stopped, as if he had said too much, and resumed more soberly. "I'll level with you. I've had Eccles in my sights for a long time, and I'm in the middle of sorting him out. I'm not going to tell you how, but it'll hit him where it hurts the most." He tapped the fax, "This would be very damaging to Eccles if it got out now." His jocularity vanished, and his eyes on Heather and me were calculating. "It wouldn't suit me either, if it became public knowledge. I don't want him running scared before I've cooked his goose. I want him innocent and trusting as a lamb. How about we keep this as our little secret for the time being?"

I sensed his power, Vin's watchful support of her boss, and Heather pulling herself out of whatever feelings she had for him.

"What about David Hall? And I need some reassurance that what you're planning for Eccles doesn't involve physical harm to him and his family." Her crisp unemotional words challenged him like a drawn blade.

He acknowledged her courage with a nod. "I'm being honest with you. I've heard nothing on the grapevine about Hall. That doesn't mean Eccles didn't have a hand in his death, especially if he knew that Hall had found him out over Berkeley Dock." He included us both in his candid gaze. "This is a violent town, and always has been. Shipbuilding is hard manual labour, and men can easily fall into drinking too much, and settling arguments with their fists. Now there's unemployment and drugs, and it's no different. You may say that I do nothing to change things, and you'd be right, I'm not a social reformer. I give people what they want, and pocket the proceeds. Violence isn't my style, though." He gave a rueful glance down at his rotund middle, "You might gain a short-term advantage from it, but it's a blunt instrument, and one that's likely to backfire. If you beat someone up, you're always going to have them hating you and egging their relatives on to do the same thing back to you. You can break people just as effectively by other means."

"Like what?" Heather sounded interested. My blood was running cold.

He grimaced, "I can see I'm going to have to tell you this. My old man was a scrappy, and strong as an ox. Jesus, could that man drink. Twenty pints a night, and that was just on weekdays, and he'd fight anything with arms that wasn't a chair. My mother was half his size, and ruled him by fear. She told him on their wedding night that if he ever raised his hand in drink to her or any children that came along, he'd have to be ready to face ground glass in his dinner, and he believed her. He wasn't a New Man, but he wasn't a bad father." He unhinged his jaw for another pastry. "Now, you'd expect him to die young from liver failure or brain damage from one fight too many, not from a broken heart, wouldn't you?"

Heather was beginning to show some sympathy. "A broken heart? Was it your mother?"

Ran shook his head. "No, his business. He rented a bit of land on the site of an old iron foundry. The land changed hands, the new owner refused to renew his lease, and it knocked the stuffing out of him. He had a stroke and faded to nothing in six months." He smiled, not very pleasantly, "No prizes for guessing who the new owner was."

"The penny's dropped," Heather said. "This is getting more like a Greek tragedy every day. If we don't interfere with your vengeful plans, will you let us in on the final denouement?"

He relaxed, and threw her a cigarette from a silver box on his desk. "It's a deal. I hope it will all be very public anyway. I'm not saying any more."

Heather clicked her lighter, "This is fun. I'd forgotten how much I enjoyed working lunches. Anything else on the agenda?"

Ran walked round the desk, and balanced an ashtray on her lap. "Only a vote of thanks to you and your paralegal for your persistance and hard work. Tell me more about your visit to Eccles Construction. I hear a gang of his carpenters have walked out."

His affability returned in full during our tale-telling. "Benson's right," he crowed, "Michael Junior is a tosser. Worse than his father, if that's possible. He's got some fancy business degree, and still couldn't manage a WI cake stall. If my plan fails, I can take comfort in the knowledge that he'll fuck up the business without trying. Clogs to clogs in three generations, as they say." He looked pleased with himself, "My boy might be a bit of a clothes horse, but he's got his head screwed on for a sixteen year old."

I poured out the last of the coffee, "Are you grooming him to take over here, for when you retire to Spain?"

He chuckled, "Hell, no. He's into sport. Doesn't drink and doesn't smoke. He wants to be a top sports psychologist, and the brains behind England winning the World Cup three times in a row, good luck to him. He goes to school and does his homework. I don't know where he gets it from."

Football. My heart tripped, and I eased my cuff up my wrist so I could see my watch without appearing rude. In less than twenty four hours, the whistle would blow for kick-off, and, barring some dreadful disaster, I would be there with Maggie. My attention wandered from Ran's description of his truant days. That bolt of attraction didn't feel like my illness coming back, it felt like a stronger version of my youthful ardour for my first proper girlfriend. Be careful, I cautioned, don't expect anything from tomorrow. Just enjoy her company, and the feeling while it lasts. If you haven't a hope with her, there may be others, now that your urge has come back.

". . .the lease was going for a song, and that's how I got started." Ran was saying. He must have noticed that I was miles away, because he broke off and smiled at me.

"Sorry, I do go on. Look, if you want to get off, I'll see Heather home. You must have things to do."

It was a gracious dismissal, and I seized it with both hands.

"That all right with you?" I asked Heather rhetorically. She was settled in with her wineglass and fags, and it would have taken a far less self-centred person than me to sacrifice a free afternoon to playing gooseberry out of concern for her well-being. Vin was already at the door.

"Absolutely. You get back to your masonry. Enjoy the football, and see you on Monday."

She wanted me to go as much as Ran did, and for a contrary second I was put out. I bloody rushed round at her beck and call, and drove her hither and thither, only to be sent packing when she had a man in her sights. Let her see what happens next time she wants a chauffeur, I thought mutinously.

She gave me a wink which Ran couldn't see. "Thank you, love," she mouthed.

Instantly contrite, I kissed her cheek. "Ring if you need a lift on Monday," I said, and went out after Vin.

"Thank Ran for the lunch," I remembered as we passed through the unlit bar.

"I will." She touched my pocket, "You wouldn't hack it as a shoplifter, I'm afraid."

"Rats. It's for my dog. There's no bottles under my jacket."

She unshot a bolt on the front door. "I'd have noticed. This David Hall business."

"Yes?"

"Ran will find out what he can. I'm not saying that you should mind your own, but don't worry about it too much."

I didn't intend to. After I'd said goodbye, I started sorting out my mental filing cabinet. David Hall, Eccles and the Berkeley Dock scandal could be locked in the bottom drawer in a file marked "Ranald MacRanald's responsibility". I was going to concentrate on not imagining what Maggie looked like without any clothes on, and on an afternoon programme of physical exercise, to ensure that I slept that night.

"What are you doing in there?" Frances grumbled outside the bathroom door on Saturday morning.

"Cutting my toenails." My programme had been too successful, I had fallen asleep again after letting Curlydog out for her not quite dawn nature call, and I was running late.

"It's a football match you're going to, not a tea dance. Hurry up, I need your help with a little job before you go."

I poked my head out of the door. "Will it take long?" I was debating whether to tempt fate by changing my sheets.

"No. Get some warm clothes on."

The wind whipped round the gable end of the barn, sprinkling us with a hint of hail.

"You've picked a good day to do this," I grunted, struggling with the extending ladders.

"It's not me who's planning on standing outside all afternoon," Frances replied through the screwdriver in her teeth. "That should do it, it's steady enough."

I kept the ladder still while she began inching upwards. I couldn't believe that she had chosen today of all days to remove the wobbly light bracket on the gable wall so that she could clean off the rust, repaint it, and put it back more securely. The ladder flexed under her weight.

"Shit." Her voice was blown away by the wind, "I can't reach it properly. My arms aren't long enough."

I didn't want her plummeting down on my head. "I'm taller. I'll have a go."

She descended with alacrity. "There's a nice view from up there."

There may have been, but with the gale drawing tears from my eyes, I couldn't appreciate it. Heights were not my favourite, and, trying not to imagine what would happen if the top of the ladder began sliding out of position, I clung with one hand to a stone protruding from the wall, and shook the iron bracket with the other. I could hear a car coming down the lane. Was it that time already?

"Take the bulb out first, dummy, and then pull out the wire," Frances shouted up. "I don't want the bulb broken."

I tweaked the bulb, and it blew out of my hand. There was a popping explosion behind me, and the sound of a car coming to an unscheduled halt. I dared to turn my head.

"Bulls-eye," Frances said. "That travelled a fair distance."

Maggie wound down the window which the bulb had hit smack on. "I wasn't expecting violence so early on. Do you try and do something hazardous every weekend?"

Chapter 13

"God, sorry," I howled into the wind. "I'm up here under duress."

"She's lying. She went up there like a monkey, so you'd be impressed. Throwing the bulb at your car was a ploy to attract your attention."

Frances had turned into a bigmouth, and I was going to pull out this bracket and brain her with it. With her hit and miss instinct she may have guessed that I was becoming keen on Maggie, but there was no call for her to broadcast it. I wrenched at the wire stapled to the bracket until it dangled free, and gave the metal an almighty tug. There was a shower of old mortar and small stones, and I swayed backwards. Maggie, out of the car by now, gave a shriek.

"I can't watch."

I looked down at the foreshortened view of her figure topped by her hat. Her hands were over her eyes. If I hurled the bracket down to fell Frances, Maggie might think it was me falling, and that wouldn't set the afternoon off on the right track.

I transferred my grip to the ladder. "It's quite safe. I'm coming down now."

I jumped the last couple of feet, and gave the bracket to Frances. "Here you are, shorty."

"Thank you Spiderwoman." "Show off," her eyes said.

I turned to Maggie. "Want a go? Look at the view?"

"Get lost. I'm wearing so many coats, I can hardly walk on the flat, and I'm not fearless like you."

"You mean you've got some sense. I didn't damage your car, did I?"

"No. I bought it from someone who lives in the Sink. The windows are bullet-proof."

We were smiling helplessly at each other, and it didn't seem forward to touch her arm.

"I'll get my jacket. I don't want to make us late."

She reached out and picked something from my hair. "Stone," she said. "Can't have you looking too rough and ready."

Abandoning Frances to wrestle with the ladder, I nearly ran to the outhouse to find my jacket.

In anyone else's company, the afternoon would have been dire. The teams were still warming up when we found a place in the stand behind one of the goals, and it wasn't a happy sight for a Millford supporter. The Wyre Rovers squad were twice as big, fit and mean as the Millford contingent, their tracksuits were smarter, and they didn't appear to have any overweight, oddly-shaped or grey-haired players. With the wind, now at hurricane strength, blowing straight in our faces, we watched them sprint in formation from one side of the pitch to the other.

"We're going to get donkey-knobbed," Maggie said. "That Reno's worth more than our entire squad, the ground and all the streets around."

"Maybe he'll get injured," I said, and wondered if my nose was getting frostbitten already. The players jogged off, the ballboys collected balls, and a foolhardly female singer in high heels emerged on to the pitch with a microphone, and tried to cajole the crowd into singing along to a number of bombastic rock anthems. In true Millford fashion, everyone groaned and chanted rude ditties instead, until, defeated by noise and the wind chill factor, she retreated in disgust. Maggie started rummaging in her bag.

"Let's start on the flask, before we die of hypothermia. I'm glad I brought all that chocolate."

We didn't see much of the first half. Wyre were attacking the goal at the other end of the pitch, so, with the action far away from us, I amused myself by watching the Wyre goalkeeper's attempts to keep warm. He ran on the spot, skipped around waving his arms, did gymnastics from the crossbar, wandered up to the half-way line and back, refused the offer of a pie from a boy standing at the front, and did some gardening on the divots in front of his goal. By half-time, Wyre were two up, to goals which I had seen only as flurries of movement followed by ecstatic hugging, and Millford supporters were beginning to applaud Reno's moves.

Maggie gave me an apprehensive look. "We'll see more in the second half." The tip of her nose was blue.

I was colder than I'd been for years, the gale was blowing coffee out of Maggie's flask cup, and a piece of chocolate snapped like an icicle into my mouth. I couldn't remember ever feeling so happy. A shifting movement of the crowd pushed Maggie against me, and I smiled with refrigerated lips.

"It's fine. It's an experience. I've never heard such a variety of swearing."

She didn't move away. "Good, isn't it. We'll have more opportunity for shouting when they're down this end."

We did. The second half passed much more quickly, and we were able to appreciate the quality of Millford's defence.

"Trip him up! Kick him!" we screamed at a sweating bow-legged youth as he chased an elegant Wyre forward. The youth fell over, the forward gave us a supercilious glare, and put in a cross. The wind picked it up, and the ball floated out of the stand.

"Nyah, you couldn't cross your eyes," Maggie declared, and switched her attention to the body on the ground. "Get up, you jessie, you're not hurt."

A minute later, the great Reno did some sweet gliding and turning, and the Millford goalkeeper was picking the ball out of the net for the third time. Then the fourth and the fifth. Reno smiled at the sportsmanlike clapping from our stand, and sauntered back to the centre circle.

"Poetry in fucking motion," a pensioner next to Maggie said. "He still loves it. Have a sweet."

The final whistle blew, and we all trooped towards the exit, like frozen peas in a bag being squeezed out of a small hole. No-one seemed angry or upset or inclined to violence. In the collective shaking of heads and mordant jokes, there was more a perverse pride that Millford had played host to such a talent, and I was now more concerned that Maggie had plans for the rest of the day, and was going to rush away as soon as she had dropped me back at the house. Fortunately, her car heater turned up full made hardly a dent in our shivering, and she seemed keen enough to accept my invitation to come in and sit on the Rayburn in the big kitchen.

"Won't your friends mind?" she asked through chattering teeth, her hands on the hotplate cover.

I stopped imagining fetching my quilt from next door, wrapping us both in it and rolling on the floor. "Frances and Philippa? Of course not. They'd positively want us to eat their cake after our ordeal."

I found the satisfyingly heavy tin, and put the kettle on. A muffled squeak and splash from the bathroom told me that the two householders had retired upstairs for the afternoon to indulge in a spot of relationship building. I envied them wholeheartedly.

Maggie politely gave no sign that she had heard. "Where's your dog?"

I glanced at the window, "In my shed, I hope. I'll go and get her, she wouldn't want to miss afternoon tea."

I roused Curlydog from the foot of my bed, threw some more logs into the smouldering stove to maintain the outhouse at a tolerable temperature, and returned to wooing Maggie with Philippa's fruitcake and pots of tea. We were on our third pot, and a technical argument about the offside rule, when Frances pottered in, looking dazed and happy.

She made for the potato sack. "Stopping for supper?" she invited Maggie casually.

Curlydog, snuffling after crumbs, wagged her tail at the magic word, and I willed myself to carry on breathing. If Maggie said no,

I wouldn't know where to put myself. She looked at me.

"I don't want to overstay. . .upset your plans. . ." I didn't think I was kidding myself in reading hope in her eyes.

"Stay, please. I'm not doing anything this evening."

Frances dropped an armful of muddy potatoes into the sink. "Yes you are. You're driving us to the pub. There's a band on." She grinned at Maggie, "Come with us. You haven't lived 'till you've been in the Black Dog on a Saturday night, and seen what happens to the gene pool when the lifeguard is missing."

I fully forgave her for her earlier indiscretion. I didn't care either that Philippa's guiding hand was probably behind the invitation, and the evening's seamless progression from a laidback supper to a noisy car ride to the pub, where she and Frances bought Maggie drinks, teased her about the number of coats she was wearing, and generally treated her like an old friend.

"They're nice," Maggie said, when they obligingly stood up to boogie on down with a couple of ancient farmers who liked a dance.

I agreed, and then remembered. "I forgot to say, Frances knows your ex."

Her eyes met mine over her beer glass, "What ex?"

I tingled all over. We were having a moment. I made my voice husky, "The one in York. She must have been out of her mind not to. . ."

"Sarah!" I nearly fell into my mineral water at the hearty clap on my shoulder, "Can't I persuade you to have one of my babies?"

It was the llama farmer, and by the time I had got rid of her, Maggie was taking off yet another sweater, Frances and Philippa were back at the table, and the band had cranked up the volume from loud to ear-splitting. Calm down, my inner pessimist ordered, it was the alcohol talking. At least this has been more like a date than a visit to the paper factory. You could try the cinema next.

At chucking out time, I decided that I wouldn't ask Maggie in for a sobering cup of coffee. Never mind that I had stoked up the stove again, and plumped up cushions on the settee, before our departure, it was far too soon to try anything on. We had weeks of working together ahead, it would be a terrible mistake to jeopardise that for an ill-timed advance when I had no idea what was going on in her mind. I would be patient and restrained, demonstrating that I wasn't a slave to off-beam impulses. Almost before I had fully stopped the car, Frances and Philippa shot out and into the house, their duty done.

"Better have a coffee before you go," I said smoothly, "that lane's bad enough when you haven't had a drink."

I thought I saw her smile. "Thanks." Her voice was matter of fact. "Those potholes are a challenge."

A blast of warm air hit us when I opened the door. Maybe I had overdone the logs. Maybe we wouldn't be able to find anything to say to one another, now that we were on our own again in a minefield of potential blunders. I didn't know if she was expecting me to leap on her, sit up all night having a deep conversation, or send her on her way after one cup of coffee and a biscuit. I waved her to the settee, and she sat down, then flew hastily upright.

"Shit! That cushion just growled at me!"

I laughed at her in relief. "Doesn't everyone have talking furniture? It's only the dog." I pulled the cushion aside, uncovering a disgruntled Curlydog. "Come on, you grumpy thing. Show Maggie your party trick."

Sensing that I needed help, Curlydog performed her sole trick with a chocolate very prettily, and jumped like a devoted lap dog on to my knees as Maggie and I sat, six inches apart, on the settee. We discussed her possible ancestry.

"Not a hint of rottweiler," Maggie concluded gravely.

I carried on tickling my ally's ears, and she groaned in slack-jawed pleasure.

"You're a softy, softy," I said. "Really, you should be chained up outside like a proper guard dog."

"You wouldn't do that with her. You're both as mushy as each other."

I didn't need to look to know that she was watching my hands. I turned to catch her eye, and she blushed. She knew that I knew. I put Curlydog carefully down on the floor.

"Sarah. It's been a nice. . .a fantastic day. . ." Her voice ran out of places to go, and the six inches shrank to nothing.

She had fine lines round her eyes and mouth, and it seemed like a good idea to follow them with my fingertips. Then it seemed like a better idea to kiss them. I still couldn't be certain, even when her hand went to the back of my neck, her lips parted gently under mine, and her tongue sent thrilling messages to parts of my body whose existence I'd all but forgotten. Was this a goodnight kiss? Did she only want a snog on the sofa? I drew back a little. She smiled a very unprofessional smile.

"Kiss me again."

All those rounded curves were in my arms, and it was a nightmare to reach the soft skin that waited. She had put every single layer back on before we left the pub, and as I encountered still another woolly barrier, I realised that she was laughing.

"What?" I panted. Her own unhurried exploration was making me ache in a way I'd thought I would never experience again.

"You're not going to believe this. I'm wearing longjohns as well."

Our eyes held. I unfastened her jeans.

"Hell, so you are."

"Unh." Her hips moved. "Gorgeous woman. Why don't we just swoosh everything off, and get into bed? I want you properly."

I gasped at the deep contraction in my belly. "Behind the curtain," I croaked.

It was a miracle that I was able to walk that far. The swooshing was blissful torment, and she laughed again when, with a moan of triumph, I finally flung the longjohns into space. Her arms curled up to bring me back to her open body.

"Ok?" I breathed. It was so long since I'd done this, I didn't want to be doing it all wrong for her.

She shuddered, "Jesus, yes." She pulled my hand towards her, I slid into liquid heat, and her cries chased all my worries away.

"Oh God," Maggie moved her face away from my shoulder, "I'm sorry. I would have fetched you some ear-plugs if I'd known."

I stroked her hair, and kissed the top of her head. "Don't be sorry, I liked it. It made it. . .even better." I didn't want her to start feeling embarrassed, and I certainly didn't want her conscience to kick in. I wanted to try it again, in case that beautiful searing explosion had been a fluke. I'd guessed that she would be nice, but I had never expected her to be so hungry, so adroit, and so deliciously giggly. Deprived of that kind of touch for an age, I wasn't ready to let her go just yet.

"Oh dear. We shouldn't have. . .I should never. . .I couldn't possibly. . ."

I ignored her words, and concentrated on what her magnificent body was saying.

"You don't have to. . ." she protested feebly. My mouth moved down her stomach. "Oh." She clutched at me. "Ah, all right, maybe I could. . .blimey, would you do that for the next half an hour or so please?"

I decided that I had been wasting my time chasing after young girls. Mature women were much more fun.

It must have been about six in the morning when furtive footsteps woke me from a satisfied doze. I reached out, and felt only bedclothes, warm and wrinkled from us together.

"Fuck," the shape by the bed whispered.

"Maggie? What are you doing? Come back to bed, it's cold."

The shape crouched down, and scrabbled for something on the floor.

"I can't. I can't stay. That was really wrong."

I stretched my legs. I felt great. "Seemed all right to me."

There was an agonised "mmf".

I sighed. I wasn't up to anything other than sleep, and selfish gloating over my return to perfect working order. "Listen, Maggie," I tried not to sound too blunt, "we haven't done anything wrong. We're two consenting adults, we fancy each other, and we did what comes naturally. There's no-one else involved, and," my tired brain laboured to pinpoint what might be her major worry, "I'm not going to make things difficult for you at work. I'm not that unstable."

"Do you mean that?" In the dark, I couldn't decipher the emotion behind her stiff question.

"Of course." I'd crept out of enough beds at dawn not to do what I would have dreaded then, and so I didn't jump up to make her stay and let me hold her until breakfast time and probably afterwards.

The curtain moved. "I'm going."

"It's up to you." I became practical, "Try not to let Curlydog out, it's too early, and she might decide to take a wander."

"Ok."

I told myself that it would make it even more awkward if I got up and kissed her goodbye. I heard her brush the curtain aside, and bump into the settee. I crushed the painful twinge in my heart.

"Maggie?"

"What?" She was barely audible.

"That was wonderful. Don't forget your longjohns."

There was a sound I interpreted as a laugh, the door opened and shut, and she was gone. Not being a particularly nice person, I hugged a pillow and instantly went back to sleep.

"Here we go again." Philippa looked up from the Sunday paper, "You've done it, haven't you? Where is she? What have you done with the poor woman? Booted her out, now you've got what you wanted?"

It was late in the morning, and I was on my way to the bathroom for a congratulatory soak.

"Poor woman nothing. She left of her own accord. Probably couldn't face the thought of the Spanish Inquisition here." I was a fully-functioning woman again, and everything was rosy.

Frances lowered the tone from behind the magazine section, "Marks out of ten?"

"Frances!" Philippa bleated.

I preened. "Easily ten and a half." The devil got hold of me, "And I'm not only talking about myself, if you get my drift."

Frances looked round the page and raised an eyebrow. I galloped headlong into damnation.

"A tenner says she's back within a fortnight."

"Make it a week."

"You're on."

I ran whistling up the stairs. I was on a high. Little did Frances know that Maggie had left a sweater and a pair of socks behind. She was bound to ring before Friday to make an arrangement to pick them up, and then who knew what could happen. She had wanted me so badly, and surely sweet-talking her out of her fit of morals wouldn't be beyond me. I would persuade her that I could be discreet, and that we might as well be hung for a sheep as for a lamb... I wriggled hedonistically in the hot water. On the other hand, now that I was obviously fit again, the world was full of possibilities. There was that promising looking woman who worked at the Borough Baths, and a trip to Manchester might be on the cards again. I sang to myself, and planned an afternoon run which would keep my ravishing body in shape, and use up some of this rampant energy.

Chapter 14

Maggie hadn't rung by Tuesday night, and I had to concede that I was getting into a state. On Monday, I was still optimistic, in a slightly more balanced way, and at the Art Project had concealed my conquest from Heather. She was gloomy again, and didn't want to talk about Ran, which had led me to conclude that they had had some uncomfortable contretemps over the weekend, the details of which she wasn't ready to disclose.

"Football nice?" she grunted, slopping textured paint on a plant pot.

"Freezing cold, force ten gale, and we lost."

"So I heard." Her hand slipped, and paint sprayed over the table. "Oh fuck it."

Over at the sewing machine, May gave a sharp intake of breath. I grabbed a handful of paper towels. I could see the frustrated tear in Heather's eye.

"No permanent damage done. Let's have a tea break."

Out by the bins, Heather looked cold and small. Her weaker hand was shaking.

"Painful today?" I asked through the impotent sympathy in my chest.

"Mm. The doctor's fiddling around with my drugs, but you know, sometimes nothing quite hits it." She shut her eyes. "It's crap, Sarah, it's crap being like this." The tear ran down her cheek.

I seized her stronger hand. I was tearing apart inside. "Sweetheart, if there was anything I could do. . ."

"But there isn't." She gripped my hand, "Apart from be here."

"I'll always try. . ."

Her grip relaxed, "I know. You're a brick." She found a tissue and blew her nose.

I cleared my throat, "When I was younger, I went on an animal rights demo. Now I'd say use as many rats as you like, clone human embryos to harvest stem cells, do anything you want if it would make things better for you."

She gave her cigarette a last drag. "Yeah, it's amazing how fragile one's ethics are. I suppose if I was a spiritual person, I'd see things differently. Find some reason behind it all."

I took her hand again. "There isn't any. Like, when I was really bad in Monk's House, I knew for certain the ultimate futility of everything. Now I sort of know it underneath, but it isn't so overwhelming, so I can get on with stuff that helps me through the day, and even enjoy some of it."

I was meant to be supporting her. This was definitely not the time to mention my re-discovery of a major compensation for being snared in existence.

She gave my fingers another squeeze, "You were quite ill, weren't you?"

I had never told her exactly what I had been like. "Oh yes. In hysterics at one point, shouting and babbling right out of my tree. I didn't eat for days. They poured liquid valium and God knows what into me. I'm amazed my constitution recovered."

"Wheesh, at least I've never been like that." I had cheered her up. "Let's get back in the warm. I think Bridie's planning a treat for us."

The treat, we soon discovered, was a bunch of the free tickets Pedersens had distributed like confetti to a rare ship launch in the yard on Wednesday morning. Bridie was enthusiastic.

"Why don't we meet up before, cheer the launch, and all have lunch together afterwards? There might be enough in the kitty for us to have the happy hour at the Italian."

This was hailed as a sound plan, and on my return home, I found myself wishing that I could ring Maggie to tell her about it, and also to inform her that Curlydog had now sampled the crocuses and a hyacinth. There was nothing to stop me picking up the phone to check that she had arrived home safely. What kind of day had she had? Perhaps she hadn't missed her sweater, or the socks which were now in the wash. They were smaller than mine, and one was wearing thin at the heel. I hoped it would survive the spin cycle. Curlydog had used the sweater as a blanket during the day, yet it still held an indefinable scent, and I hid it, neatly folded, out of her reach. I looked at the phone. No, I wouldn't rush her. There was plenty of time before Friday.

On Tuesday, after a restless night, I applied myself in the garden, and finished my wall. Frances and Philippa declared it a fine piece of handiwork, toasted me with mugs of tea, and talked about building a covered walkway between the outhouse and the loo in the yard.

"It could be quite a feature, with trellises for plants," Philippa said, her eyes narrowed in thought. "It's not fair on you that you have to walk through all that mud. I'll do a design, and Frances can say if it's practical."

I smiled, told them my current arrangements were no bother, and wanted Maggie to be there, so that she could see what I had built. The phone remained obstinately silent all evening. She could be playing football, and expecting to see me at the Borough Baths, not knowing that Frances had booked a squash court for Thursday instead. Then she might go on for a drink with her friends, damn her. There she was, carrying on with her normal life, as if nothing had happened. She clearly didn't give a fig for me. She had been willing to use me when the fancy took her, but I wasn't good enough for a longer term arrangement, because I'd been in Monk's House, and she was on the staff. How could she be so self-centred, callous, unwilling to take risks and...utterly gorgeous and desirable? Perturbed, Curlydog stared at me from my lap as I pretended to read on the settee, and wiggled her tail uncertainly.

"Maggie doesn't want to know us any more," I said into her wise eyes.

She gave a little whine, and I buried my face in her wiry coat.

"I know. I've got you. Let's go for a walk, and then have a midnight feast without the cats."

Tormented by dreams of Maggie's limbs melting into mine, I slept even more badly that night, and it was a huge effort to drive into Millford for the ship launch. My head ached, it was hell finding a parking space, and the car was making a funny noise. If Heather was still depressed, I thought, I would suggest we stood at the bottom of the slipway, and let the ship put an end to our problems. She, however, had her brave face on, and was being heroically interested in William's list of all the ships he had seen being launched while he insisted on pushing her chair. At a snail's pace, we joined the throng snaking unevenly to the yard gates, overtaken by crocodiles of primary school children dutifully carrying small flags, and shepherded by harassed yet smiling teachers.

"Come on my little flock," I heard one of them say as the waist-high heads bobbled past. "If we make the launch late, the ship will stick in the mud, and all our names will be in the crime column of the Gazette."

"Oh Miss," a child hanging on to her hand laughed in delighted fear, "they won't will they?"

I looked at the clear faces. Here they were, children in cheap trainers from a technically deprived area stuffed with broken homes and no doubt abusive adults, yet most of them trotted along as if life was all a morning off school. Sentimental twit, I scolded myself, they probably know more swear words than you do. It was almost impossible, however, not to be caught up in the buzz, as what looked like most of Millford's population funnelled through the yard gates, and swarmed to the best vantage points, and I found myself doing a country bumpkin gawp at all the people, the buildings, and the water at the foot of the sloping yard.

"Wheelchair coming through," William foghorned, and we pushed sheepishly through to the front.

On the decks of the ship, massive and precarious on its concrete supports, minute red-hatted figures spoke into walkie-talkies, giving the crowd an occasional wave.

"You know what their job is?" William informed us. "When the ship hits the water, they have to rush below, and check for leaks."

We didn't know whether to believe him or not.

"Hope they're wearing life-jackets," Heather remarked. "Get that hat."

A line of dignitaries was processing up a makeshift stairway to a covered dais at the ship's bow, and a long-skirted woman tried to rein in the wagon-wheel of felt and gauze on her head, whilst stopping her dress blowing off. A piercing longing for Maggie to be giggling with us cramped my chest. She would have appreciated the odd archaism of the amplified prayers for the ship and its crew, and the way we rhubarbed through the National Anthem while May's booming soprano caused more than one head to turn. I only forgot her in the agony of tension after the champagne smashed against the grey steel, and the huge shell remained motionless for a hung second. Then it began moving. The boiler-suited men next to us, previously quiet, released a desperate growl, as if urging their creation into life. Tugs blared, the ship picked up speed, hit the rising tide in a crash of water, and floated high into the arms of its cables. For a few seconds, I looked back at the not very pretty town, and thought I understood it.

"This is the last ship on their books which they're going to launch like this," Bridie said, "I'm glad we saw it."

William wiped the corner of his eye with a gnarly finger, "Aye. Thank the lord I won't be around when they stop building ships in this town."

May scoffed, "Hark at you, old-timer. You've another twenty years in you yet. Let's get some garlic bread in you, put some petrol in your engine."

He winked at us. "You've a hope. Me crankshaft's busted. It'd take more than garlic to get me going."

They heckled at each other all the way to the Italian.

Not much profitable work got done in the Art Project that afternoon. We sat round, egging on William and May to tell us scandalous stories from the old days, and putting the world to rights. May, with the benefit of a glass of wine in the Italian, expounded her philosophy.

"You're a long time dead. I've buried two husbands, and I'd marry again if I found the right man. It's never too late to enjoy yourself. Mind, it's better nowadays, all free and easy, neighbours don't turn their noses up at you in the street if you have a friend stop over."

"May, you don't." Heather seemed aghast.

"Why should young people have all the fun? Not that men my age are much cop, though. Don't look too good with their teeth out, and their scraggly little. . ."

"Stop there!" we shouted.

"Necks, I was going to say. What a dirty-minded lot you are."

Before we left, I had decided to ring Maggie that evening. It was silly, hanging on like this, not communicating, and not knowing how she was after those hours of closeness. At least I could find out if she wanted us to be friends, and reassure her that we could still work together.

"How are you getting home?" I asked Heather, holding the door open with one foot, and helping her out of the building.

"Where's your car?"

I thought. "Miles away. I had to park in the long-stay at the other end of town."

"I'll ring for a taxi. Let's wait in that grassy bit round the corner."

I pushed her while she spoke into her phone. The afternoons were definitely getting lighter, and now that I'd finished the wall, I could start digging over vegetable beds, consulting Philippa on our rotation system, and setting off seeds in the greenhouse. It might be a nice change to try some different varieties of new potato, perhaps we should send off for a few catalogues. An ambulance with tinted windows drew up to the kerb alongside us, and a man in a fluorescent waistcoat over green overalls jumped out. He was blocking our way, and I swerved the chair.

"Excuse me. . ." He didn't move. "Excuse me," I repeated louder.

"We're your transport," he said.

Heather looked up from slipping her phone into her bag. "No you're not. I didn't order an ambulance."

He stood there, breathing through his mouth. He had sparse brown hair and broken veins on his nose, and looked out of shape for a member of the emergency services.

"You've got one." He pulled a piece of paper from his pocket, "Heather Shaw. To the hospital, to see the consultant."

Heather shook her head, "Sorry mate, you're wrong. I haven't got an appointment. Your dispatcher must have cocked up. Give them a ring and check."

I came out of my day dream of offering tiny new potatoes, fresh from the ground and covered with mint and butter, to Maggie. I recognised that voice. A warning gong rattled my brain-pan.

"Heather, he's not an ambulance man. He works for Eccles." My voice was shockingly wavery. I reversed the chair to spin Heather round, and run off in the opposite direction. I couldn't be mistaken. He was the look-out who had wanted a pee when I was snooping with Curlydog in Berkely Dock.

Another fluorescent waistcoat barred my way. "Don't be awkward. Let's do this nice and calm, like. Don't want to cause a scene."

He wasn't quite seven foot tall, and he didn't have a baseball bat, but he was definitely the heavy who had chased us. In daylight I could see that his head was shaved, revealing a tattoo across his skull, and that he recognised me. Cold sweat bathed my face, and black dots danced in front of my eyes. This was it. We were going to end up like David, washed ashore on Trotters Bank, after hours of pain and hopeless suffering. My depression had been right, an accurate foretelling that I had no future...

"Yeah, right." Heather's voice was dead-pan. "We're going to toddle off with you two jokers. I'll just check that Mrs Stupid is at home today."

I stopped myself whimpering, and concentrated on keeping my feeble lips shut. There was no point in struggling, Heather would find that out sooner or later, it would be better to get this over and done with. The two men exchanged looks and nods, and the one in front of us put his hand in his overall pocket. When he withdrew it, I saw the dull sheen of a blade.

"All right, little lady. I can spoil your good looks. And your fucking dog-walking friend's."

Heather's derision quaked my spine. "What good looks? Could I be worse off than I am now? You'd be doing me a favour. Here," she thrust out her arms, wrists upwards, "go for the arteries. I'd do it myself if I wasn't so squeamish. Bleeding to death on the street wouldn't be bad, compared with rotting in this chair."

This wasn't in his script. He licked his lips, and latched on to me.

"Your friend doesn't look so sure."

I tried to match Heather's contempt. "I've got clinical depression. I don't give a fuck what you do. Saves me cutting myself." That was the biggest lie I had told in my life, and I mutely asked forgiveness from the people in Monk's House who did just that.

His lip curling, he sneered at Heather, "You're taking the piss. You're fucking coming with us, spazzer."

The playground insult halted the intellectual processes which had been telling me that he was cracking, and that we were going to talk our way out of this. All the destructive rage I had kept a jumping lid on in the worst phase of my illness burst like a geyser. I twisted round, and landed a mighty kick on the man behind me, exactly where it would hurt the most. My aim was true, there was a horrid cry, and the flabby body doubled up, then collapsed on all fours. I whirled round again. I had that damn length of twine in my hands, and I was going to loop it round that bastard's neck, and twist it tight. The knife flashed up, and met a wall of sound.

Heather had set off her rape alarm. Windows opened along the street, a car stopped in its tracks a few yards away, and a cat screeched past, its fur stiff as a brush. We froze in a confused tableau. A door squeaked behind me, and, in double vision, I saw our would-be kidnapper run to his mate, drag him into the ambulance, scramble into the driver's seat, and gun off, narrowly missing the stationary car. Heather switched off the alarm, the car drove slowly past, and I was sitting on the pavement, my face between my knees, straining for breath and sanity.

A light pressure on the back of my neck made me look dizzily up. Two pairs of elderly eyes studied me. Luckily, they belonged to two different people.

"Don't kick me. Your friend's saying they weren't ambulance men. Should we call the police?" He had his slippers on, and his hands were hovering protectively over the front of his trousers. His wife was still holding a dish-cloth.

Heather wheeled herself unevenly closer, "They were trying to mug us. I've got a taxi coming. We'll go to the police station ourselves." She was cool and unaffected. "Thank you for coming out. Sorry about the disturbance."

He moved his hands, eyeing me more kindly. "Are you sure? Shouldn't you have some hot sweet tea? You come inside, we'll put the kettle on."

"No, really. I'm a solicitor. The police will be in touch if they need witnesses. What number house are you? And your names, if that's all right with you." She gathered information as if she was in her office. "Here's the taxi. Thank you again."

My fingers thick and clumsy, I went through the wheelchair routine, and fell into the back seat. I had a bad case of drunken legs. The police might not be convinced that booting someone in the balls was legitimate self-defence, and I could be in a lot of trouble. I had never lost my temper like that before. What if it had made things worse, and Heather had been hurt? What if it started happening regularly? I should see the psychiatrist again.

"The Big Top," Heather said to the driver. She tried to move her head round so that she could see me. "Wow, that was phenomenal, you big heroine, you. I might change my mind about you." She was whispering.

"Too late," I whispered back. "I think I love Maggie." The driver could probably hear, and I didn't care.

She inspected me, and I grasped that the coolness was an act. "Yes. I didn't want to get knifed or die, not with them, like that."

"Nor me." I was going to cry, and that was something I never did. "We're not going to the police?"

"Of course not. That's one complication we don't need. Hold on, we'll soon be safe."

"You'll be fine, you'll be fine," Vin repeated, her hand steady on my knee. The coffee mug shook in my fist, and brown liquid slopped to the floor.

"I lost it. I lashed out. I'm a thug."

"That makes two of us."

"I was out of control."

"It's in all of us, when we're under threat. You did the right thing. I think even Ran would have had a go if he'd been there. I've never seen him so irate."

My shakes were retreating, and I lit a cigarette. I couldn't quite believe that we'd nearly been abducted in broad daylight. My aching toes reminded me that it hadn't been a hallucination.

"Lucky that old couple came out. I was on my way to garotting the other bloke."

Vin laughed. "That was Gnasher Bell, from your description. He could do with a little strangling."

"Gnasher?"

"He eats beer glasses. He's banned from here."

"He must be rough. . .hell, sorry, that came out wrong."

She was only more amused. "He is. Not the brightest spark in the battery, either. I think it's the thought of him in particular threatening Heather that's got Ran's goat."

I drank without missing my mouth. I was calming down. The look of polite disapproval on Ran's face when we burst into his office had changed through incomprehension to one of monstrous anger as we blurted out our story. The veins on his forehead had bulged like snakes, until Heather, her competence derailed, had burst into tears. He had scooted to her chair, and, stumbling after Vin to this corner of the bar, I had left them to it.

"Vin? Sarah?" Ran was pushing Heather through to us, "I've changed my mind. To the car! We're going to put a stop to this nonsense."

Chapter 15

I drove towards Byreby, framed by the searching headlights of Ran's BMW. His plan was not elaborate. A call to Eccles Construction had told him that its owner had left for home, and apparently our strategy was to confront him at the Hacienda, and bully him into contrition. I had vague premonitions of shouting, threats, and anti-social behaviour from Vin, who had practised chief bouncer expressions on the way to the car, but oddly enough, I was no longer a quivering meringue of fear. I had calmly suggested that I should pick up my car, and that we should all stop at Frances and Philippa's on the way, so that I could feed Curlydog, and now I was driving perfectly capably. Heather had insisted on coming in my car, with the excuse that we both needed to get back our confidence in being alone, yet I knew the real reason.

"You're about to explode," I said. "Go on, ask me what you're dying to know."

"What can you mean? Hm, yes, you did let slip a little remark which led me to believe that, oh clever me, I was right about you and a certain occupational therapist, and, perish the thought, you were wrong, wrong, wrong." She poked my leg three times. "So, tell me everything. What's been going on? Is your love returned?"

It was almost a relief to be thrown into this deep end, and not have to talk about the afternoon.

"I don't know. Yes, no, I don't think so, or maybe it's too much for her that I was a patient. She stayed with me on Saturday night, and then rushed off, and she hasn't rung, and I was going to ring her tonight, and now I'm not sure that's a good idea, and I really want to speak to her, and what do you think?"

"She stayed with you? Is that a euphemism for going the whole hog?"

"Um, yes, actually." I shifted down a gear as we came to a steep bendy bit of road. "It might mean nothing to her, or she might be regretting it, or she might be waiting for me to ring her first. What should I do?"

"You had sex?"

"Yes, I told you. Help me, give me some good advice, what chance do you think I've got of persuading her I'm sane now. . . ?"

"Was it nice?"

"Heather! Behave, I'm looking for guidance here."

I didn't get any. She spent the rest of the short drive tittering like a schoolgirl, and trying to worm details from me.

This preoccupation, pleasanter for her than for me, ended when our little calvacade drew up in the yard. I had intended a brief stop long enough only to feed the dog, but as soon as my back was turned, and I was in the outhouse with Curlydog dancing round her bowl, I realised that Philippa had come out of the back door, and the others were leaving Ran's car and helping Heather into the kitchen. Any hope I had of keeping my recent and peculiar activities secret from Frances and Philippa was now in smithereens. I hid for as long as I could, before crossing into the kitchen and facing the music.

"This is absurd," Philippa was ranting, "it's not the Wild West, you can't just go galloping off to that house like it's the OK Corral. Heather, you're a solicitor, you know that you should call the police. You could have been seriously hurt, and as for you," she caught sight of me slinking in, "why didn't you tell us any of this? You could have been murdered in your bed, and we wouldn't know." I didn't think she grasped that Ran was not your average law-abiding type, who looked to the police to deal with others' misdemeanours.

Surprisingly, Vin came to my rescue. "Sarah didn't want to bother you, in case this was a storm in a tea-cup. We're not going to beat up Eccles, or anything. We're only going to let him know that we're wise to him, and he'll stop his shenanigans. With his standing, he's got too much too lose."

Philippa seemed mollified, although I wasn't convinced that Vin was being one hundred per cent honest. She looked in the mood for breaking a few limbs and ornaments, while Ran was staring around with naked interest. It was unlikely that any of his social circle dried their clothes above the Rayburn, or had photos of tepees on the wall.

"That's some dresser," he said out of the blue. "Where did it come from?"

"I made it." Frances was gruff and suspicious.

He didn't over-enthuse. He stood up, and ran his hand down its side, and over the carved vine leaves creeping over the shelves.

"Nice job. How much do you charge for this kind of thing?"

Frances shrugged. "Depends. What kind of wood, what size, how much carving."

He nodded. "Mustn't sell yourself short." He stroked a smooth edge again. "Did you learn this type of joint in Wales? You don't see it often up here."

He had won Frances over. The two of them started a woodworking discussion, and Vin asked Philippa about her hyacinths. It was almost turning into a normal social call, and soon the kettle was boiling, Heather and Vin had a cat apiece on their laps, and, my sense of doom lessening, I had let Curlydog through to join the party. Perched on the window seat, I rationalised, putting the day's brush with danger to a reality check. Yes, it looked like Eccles had set his men on us, but, as anyone would have to admit, pensioned-off ambulance aside, it had been an extraordinarily clumsy attempt to snatch us from the street. Perhaps it had been intended merely to frighten us, and there had been no plan to whisk us away and pour us into the foundations of a new housing estate, or leave us marooned on a sandbank as the tide came in. It would be difficult to pass off our demise as an accident, if witnesses behind those closed doors had heard the commotion, and glimpsed through their net curtains to see us being carried kicking and screaming into an emergency vehicle in out of date colours. Not that I had been wrong in letting fly at that man. It had been a natural adrenalin reaction, and I shouldn't take it, or my shakes afterwards, too seriously. There, I was sorted, and not at all reluctant to go to the Hacienda, and thumb my nose at Eccles.

My bravado increased once I was sitting in the back of Ran's car, sandwiched between Vin and an uncharacteristically ebullient Frances. She and Philippa had entered so much into the spirit of our mission, that we had only persuaded Philippa to stay behind by giving her the role of back-up, with instructions to call the police if she hadn't heard from us within an hour. The engine purred, dials glowed as if on a flight deck, and superior suspension made a nonsense of our primitive track.

"Jesus, this is more comfortable than our sitting room," Frances said, stretching her legs in our luxury bubble. "Bet it cost more than most houses in Millford."

Ran piloted us out on to the road, pride oozing from every pore. "You'd have to knock together a good few dressers to pay for it."

"How nice not to worry about global warming." She couldn't resist a little dig.

"We're car-sharing aren't we? I do my bit, I've got shares in a wind farm. Your solid fuel stoves release more greenhouse gases in a year than a Concorde flight. It's fact."

"It's a load of cobblers. The ozone layer wasn't shrinking when everyone burned wood and coal."

"You had smog. That was a killer."

"So's acid rain."

Heather stirred in the front. "Is this an environmental summit, or what? Do we have any clue what we're going to do when we get to the house?"

"Let me do the talking." Ran's silky voice was merciless, his urbanity a cover for the amoral avenger underneath. Yet he must think a lot of Heather to disrupt his scheme of lulling Eccles into a false sense of security. I wondered why they had fallen out at the weekend, and why Heather had still turned to him the moment we hit trouble. In the chill of his hard purpose, I fretted once more over where their friendship could go. Of course, I was such a raving success at relationships, I would be there to guide Heather round all those pitfalls. . . I grimaced at myself, and ruminated on whether I could ring Maggie after this confrontation, without ever mentioning any of it. It was enough that I had been in Monk's House, she didn't need to know that I was involved in such lurid goings-on."

"This is it," Frances tapped Ran's shoulder. "Up the drive."

Lights were on, and whoever was inside would have had plenty of time to barricade the doors and load their shotguns while Heather swapped to her chair with everyone trying to help, and making the procedure twice as complicated as usual. We advanced to the front porch in a spearhead formation; Ran in the lead in a Mafia-don overcoat, Vin pushing Heather on his heels, and Frances and I bringing up the rear. Out of the car, I was not so brave.

"Should I have brought my big chisel?" Frances asked me, solidly unconcerned by the menace I felt leaking from the white walls and black upstairs windows of the house. Gnasher Bell could be behind that bush, or in the shadow of that wall, bat in one hand and blade in the other, a one-man frenzy of violence. My ear caught the echo of a step and breathing in the darkness. I looked compulsively round, and saw nothing. Frances' arm was across my back.

"Sheep in the field next door, I think. Anyway, you're a fast runner. Leg it if there's any trouble, and phone Philly." Her phone slipped into my pocket. She wasn't so calm after all, she never used her pet name for Philippa in public.

Ran stopped at the door, checked that we hadn't deserted him, and rang the bell. And rang and rang.

"There's definitely someone there," he muttered, "I can hear footsteps." He put his eye to the peephole in the stained wood studded with mock-baronial lumps of metal. "Michael Junior. What a pleasure."

"Go away." The invisible voice had a whiny edge. "We're calling the police."

Ran knelt down, and spoke through the letterbox. "Please do. I want to speak to them about your employees' assault on my solicitor today. Not to mention your father's misuse of public money to enrich himself, and his involvement in David Hall's death. Isn't he here?"

"No. And he wouldn't waste his breath on Sink trash like you."

"And I'm not wasting mine on insults. Use your tiny brain to give your old man a message. If he, or Gnasher Bell, or any other thugs come within a mile of my solicitor or her friends, the editor of the Gazette will be the first to know where the money for Berkeley Dock went. And you'd better hire bodyguards. Do you understand?"

He hadn't raised his voice more than was necessary to be heard through the letterbox, yet Frances shivered beside me.

There was no reply. Ran stood up and dusted his knees.

"Oh dear. You had your chance."

He barely glanced at Vin. She left Heather's chair, picked up one of the rigidly pruned shrubs which flanked the wall, and casually tossed it, ceramic pot and all, through the nearest window. Noise tore the quiet night apart. An explosive crash, a bleating stampede of sheep in the field, a scream from inside the house, and the minor popping of a final piece of glass falling to the ground. My hands were still over my ears, and Ran was kneeling at the letterbox again.

"Do you understand? There's a fair number of plants out here."

"Yes." It was a choked, unwilling cry.

"Good. You'd better ring for a chippy then, to board up that window. You don't know who might get in. Bad men from Millford will come out specially once they hear it's broken."

My shakes had come back, and I found it hard to look at Vin. She went back to Heather's chair, and started turning her round.

"Accidents happen," she said. "I was moving it out of the way of this, tripped, and, whoops, there it was, in the house. I'll pay for the window, of course."

"Lucky the curtains were drawn across that window, or it could have been very nasty." Heather's breathing wasn't quite under control.

Vin smiled. "You're sharp. I've worked with Ran for a long time. I know when he wants to make a point."

Frances stood in Ran's way. "Would it look bad if I offered to knock up some boarding for a quick fifty quid?"

"Yes." He took her arm, and made her walk back towards the car. "I can guess you disapprove. Some people only listen when they're forced to."

I found my voice. "What if he retaliates?"

"My clubs are well-insured." He relaxed into his usual front. "Good thing he lives out of the village, and the alarms didn't go off. He's not a nice man, it's only a window, and Evadne's not the sort to have a heart attack. Let's get out of here, just in case they do get silly and ring the law."

We were very efficient in helping Heather into the car, and a lot quieter in the back.

"What happens now?" Heather broke a tense silence.

Ran half turned, and I saw his reassuring grin. "I'm speeding up my timetable. Do you want to come on board? I can always use extra legal advice."

I kept quiet. This was between them, and up to Heather. I couldn't warn her not to touch his timetable with a barge-pole, or protest that the closer she became to him, the further she was moving away from me. I didn't want to spend more time with people who used threats and destruction as reasoning tools, but I couldn't speak for her.

"Tell me more." Heather had crossed an invisible line.

"We'll have a conference. Need to get you home for some supper first."

She let him take charge and exclude me, and I didn't know whether to be sorry or glad.

Ran dropped Frances and me off with an exhortation not to lose any sleep over the evening's drama, and we stood in the familiar peace of the back yard. Light from the kitchen illuminated the crocuses Curlydog had spared, and I could smell woodsmoke and cooking. A distant owl hooted on its own concerns, a fox barked, and the safe indifference of the nocturnal countryside enveloped us.

Frances opened the door, "Quite a day for you, eh? Supper sounds like a good idea."

After an hour of Philippa's cossetting, I was restored. With Curlydog pressed against my leg, I went over and over the past few weeks, and let Philippa tell me off for not confiding in them earlier.

"Of course, no-one in the village likes the Eccleses," she veered off at a tangent. "They tried to take the farmer who owns the field next to them to court, because one of his cows leaned over the wall and nibbled a tree. And they complained about mud and cowpats in the lane from where he took them backwards and forwards for milking, and the noise of the silage cutters when they kept going at night. I heard that the magistrates said it was the most frivolous waste of court time they'd ever come across, and landed Eccles with whacking great costs. Everyone will be pleased he's had a window broken, so at least you've got local opinion on your side. Not that I can condone what Vin did, or you and Heather mixing with the Millford underworld. Give me your solemn word that you won't do any more spying or karate-kicking."

"I didn't plan to do it. Why didn't you give me this dirt on Eccles before?"

"You didn't ask. You're still no closer to finding out what happened to poor David either, are you?"

I stroked Curlydog. "I have an idea." Gnasher Bell's ambulance trick had made me think. "David had a phobia about going in any form of transport. If Eccles, or someone working for him, had tried to force him into a vehicle, to talk or to threaten him, he could have panicked, and run off along the beach and into one of those awful channels."

Frances gave me a thumbs-up. "It's a workable theory. Will Heather tell you what that Ranald is planning for Eccles?"

"I doubt it. She can be very..." I wasn't sure whether I had intended to say bloody-minded or discreet, but I was cut off by the sound of a car coming into the yard. Eccles or the law. I sprang to my feet. I could sprint upstairs, and hide in the attic, or climb out of the sitting room window, and take to the woods.

Philippa smiled benevolently. "This'll be Maggie. She rang when you were both off breaking windows, and said she'd pop round. I forgot to tell you."

"You what?" How could she have forgotten something so vital? My heart bounced like a firecracker from shock to delight to apprehension and back again, and I could feel the blush racing from my neck to the roots of my hair. Play it cool, I thought, she was the one who rang first, just get her out of the kitchen and on her own. Then she was on the threshold, beautiful, real and spitting feathers.

"Hi, hi," she gave Frances and Philippa the obligatory greeting, and unbent enough to pat Curlydog. I could tell she wanted to shout, but I was unable to stop grinning.

"Come through to the back," I said, "I'll fetch your things."

Philippa, bless her, had tended to my stove while I was otherwise occupied, and the outhouse was as hot as my face.

"Do you want your socks? I washed them." When I had discovered what was bugging her, I would have more of a chance of putting it right. She must have been working late, she was still in her long grey skirt and smart jacket, and her ankles were neater than I remembered.

"Socks?" She was as pink as I was, "How could you?"

"I thought you'd like them freshly laundered."

"Not them!" She was yelling, and Curlydog and I jumped with fright. "How could you be mixed up in something so serious, and not tell me? You could have been killed, and I wouldn't find out until I read it in the Gazette." Philippa had been talking. "I know sex doesn't mean much to you, and you only wanted a one-night stand, but..."

I was equally outraged. "I never said that! You're the one who doesn't want to take things further because I'm an ex-patient. You don't want to be involved with me, so why should I tell you everything I do?"

"I never said that!"

"So why did you rush off?"

"You would have kicked me out in the morning."

"No I wouldn't."

"Yes you would. You didn't ring."

"Neither did you."

Curlydog joined in, pointing her nose to the ceiling, and barking joyfully.

"Oh shut up," Maggie snapped. "Mind your own business."

"Leave my dog alone," I snapped back. "She can bark if she wants."

The angle of Maggie's jaw altered, and she took a step sideways. "Oh dear." Her shoulders were wobbling.

"I'm glad you find it amusing that I've been so upset." I didn't sound half as aggrieved as I intended.

She held on to the back of the settee for support. "It's not you. I've been at a conference all day. I rang here before the closing session." She tried to compose herself and doubled up. "It was on anger management, hur, hur, hurgh."

In appreciation, Curlydog stopped barking, ran over to her, rolled on her back, and waved her legs in the air.

"You traitor," I said.

In the sudden peace, we looked at each other properly. Maggie scuffed her eyes with her wrist.

"You were upset?"

"Mm."

"Oh." She crouched down, and rubbed Curlydog's stomach.

"Um," I had to glean some indication of where this left us, "I, er, I'm missing you." It took more courage to say that than it had to kick Eccles' man.

She was finding Curlydog fascinating, and my shoulders drooped. "Ah well, never mind. I'll get your sweater and socks."

She let me get as far as the curtain. "Sarah. Forget the bloody socks. That's not why I came."

"No?" I found I was fingering the velvet, and made a conscious effort to stop.

"No. I was frightened for you. And I've been mad at you, and mad at myself."

"Why?" It was only two strides to reach the settee, and rest on the arm.

Her downturned face was vulnerable. "It's not such a big issue that you were in Monk's House. I just don't want to be a notch on your bedpost." The words sounded as if they were being extracted from her with pliers.

I couldn't believe that I had contemplated pursuing any other woman. "You were never that."

Her head came up, and I saw confusion, relief and the beginnings of uncertain pleasure in her eyes. "Are you just saying that?"

"No. Why would I?" My heart was going nineteen to the dozen, and my legs had fallen into some kind of swoon.

She had a dimple when she smiled. "Because you've got that look on your face."

The ache had returned. "What look?" She was teasing me, and I was elated.

She stood up, dropping her jacket to the floor. "The look that says you want to do this."

She moved easily into my arms, and Curlydog sighed and pattered off to her box.

Chapter 16

"You're not leaving this time." I anchored Maggie to the bed with my arm.

She bit my ear, very softly. "I only want the loo."

I kissed her dimple, her chin, and the creamy hollow of her neck. "What a nuisance you are. That means I have to move."

"'Fraid so."

She didn't hurry to disentangle herself, and we slipped in a few more kisses before I rolled out of bed, wrapped her in my old coat, and handed her the torch I used for such occasions.

"I'm sorry it's so primitive. Don't get lost."

"I'll bring my own chamber pot next time. Come and look for

me if I'm not back in ten minutes."

She inched out of the door, and I jumped back under the quilt. Next time. I felt like Curlydog must have done when she found a box of chocolates and scoffed the lot, leaving only a pile of shredded silver paper and soggy cardboard to tell of her orgy. It had been different tonight, and although I wasn't ready to put it into words with Maggie, I knew she had felt it too, from the way she had kept her gaze fixed on mine, and the way we had held each other afterwards. I stretched my arms and rotated my ankles. I must be nearly better. A day like today, and I could still lose myself in lovers' talk and a willing body. There was a shimmy of cold air, and Maggie was beside me again, pressing her icy feet against mine.

"Yow," I rubbed her chilled flesh, "living in a shed isn't all log fires and romance."

She buried her nose in my shoulder. "I'm not complaining. If you were to offer me some refreshment now, you'd be the perfect hostess."

I apologised again. "I didn't think. Didn't you get supper on your very effective anger management thing?"

Her legs were warming up and snaking round mine. "A bit. Though a cup of tea and a biscuit would slip down very nicely."

This cushioned flesh was far more exciting than bony ribs and hard shoulder blades. "I'm out of practice. I've never entertained like this here."

Her lips paused. "Really?" There was surprise under the light question.

"Really." I was drawn to make it clear, "You're the first since I was ill. Did you think you weren't?"

"Yes."

Somehow we had shifted position, and begun to murmur.

"It's been ages for me as well." It was both a confession and an invitation.

I moved with her delicate hands, "But you're so sexy. . ."

She gave one of her delighted giggles. "And your thighs are to die for. . . Let's postpone the tea for a moment."

I sipped my coffee, "Use the shower in the house, then you can go straight to work, and won't have to rush."

Maggie looked shocked. "I can't do that! They'll know what we've been doing."

I laughed at her prissy expression. "They'll know anyway. They'll have been listening out for your car leaving all night, and will draw their own conclusions. I'm surprised Philippa hasn't been in already with some weird excuse. I think I can hear her footsteps now."

"God, no, how mortifying." She tried to shrink under the quilt, then registered the absence of noise. "You nasty thing."

"Mind my coffee."

I was perturbed, I could seriously get used to this. Waking up to her had been an erotic novelty and strangely comfortable all at the same time, and I wanted more mornings when I could watch her emerge from sleep into happy consciousness of what I was doing. I didn't know whether I could safely assume that this was going to be a regular occurrence or not, nor did I trust myself to say the right thing. Maggie jumped in where I feared to tread.

"Hypothetically speaking, if you were my girlfriend, would you come with me to the pub quiz next week to make up our team?" She spoke over the rim of her mug, concentrating on the middle distance.

I seized the opening. "Hypothetically speaking, yes."

She relaxed. "Good. It's on Thursday evening."

I put my arm back round her shoulders. "I want to keep on seeing you." Maybe that wasn't flowery enough.

"That's a relief."

Neither of us was quite prepared to venture further, and she changed the subject with a slight kick.

"You still haven't told me anything about this trouble you're in."

I put my mug down, and decided to kiss her again. "How about tonight? I'll tell you everything."

"Er," she made a feeble attempt to push me away, "I've got stuff to do at home, and sleep to catch up on. Stop, I really really have to go."

"The weekend?" I took an enormous risk, "You could bring your toothbrush over on Friday, and we could. . . hang out together."

She was suddenly very still. Dammit, I thought, I should at least have suggested taking her out somewhere appropriate.

I floundered on, "Did you have other plans? Would you rather do something else?" I needed a guide to modern dating procedures.

Her stillness broke, and her arms were round my neck. "Of course I wouldn't rather do something bloody else. Do you think I get offers like this every week? As long as I'm not invading your privacy."

"Invade it all you like. . . will you get the sack if you're late for work?"

"Aw, Heather, can't you even give me a teeny weeny hint?" My pestering hid the fact that I was pleased at Heather's arrival as usual at the Art Project on Monday, and again today for the Wednesday session. Whatever Ran was cooking up with her, he wasn't monopolising her entirely, and I wasn't so absorbed with Maggie that I wanted our friendship to fade along with the traumas of the previous week.

Heather smiled through her fog of smoke. "I'm sworn to secrecy. It's a bind, though, because I'm dying to tell you. Ran is being very clever, completely non-violent and almost legal. I'm trying to get you a walk-on part, so you'll find out, when we're ready to roll. Besides," she went on the offensive, "you haven't told me anything about you and Maggie, apart from being all gooey on Monday because you spent the weekend together. Are you definitely going out with her?"

"I don't know. I think we're taking it one day at a time. She's meant to be coming round tonight." I had been looking forward to this almost since she left on Monday morning, which now seemed ages ago, even though we'd spent an hour on the phone last night. Over a weekend of long hours in bed, a little walking and gardening, and a lot of eating and easy chatting with Frances and Philippa in the kitchen, I hadn't once felt stifled or cramped by Maggie's presence, and she hadn't run away when I told her about Eccles. The only difficult moment had been when Frances had slipped me a tenner, and I'd had to pretend that it was for some varnish I'd bought. Maggie fitted perfectly into my domestic life, and I was scared. Scared that if I sat her down and spelt out what a liability my depression was, I would frighten her away, and scared that if we carried on avoiding the subject, we wouldn't progress beyond jokes and affectionate lust. It's terrible, I told myself, you finally want that dreaded thing, a relationship. Perhaps it's one of your symptoms, and once Maggie finds out how desperate you are, she'll be off like a shot.

Heather made a "phoo" sound through her nose. "Sounds pretty full on to me. How did it go, working with her on Friday?"

"It was fine." We had been very smooth; model professionals in the group, and snatching an anticipatory snog behind a screen in the empty room after everyone had gone.

Heather phooed again. "See. How much are you telling me? I'll let you in on one thing, though. Ran's being what he calls creatively petty. He's discovered how to clog up Eccles Construction's computer with masses of e-mails that look proper but take ages to download, so that should keep the receptionist of the year busy. And Vin keeps sending dubious characters round to the Hacienda with offers to tarmac the drive and pebble-dash the walls. If you can think of anything else, let me know."

I considered some of the annoyances of modern living. "Double-glazing and kitchen salesmen? Those pushy guys who try to con you into changing your utility company?"

Heather looked more fulfilled than I had ever seen her. "All possibilities. I'm trying to contrive a snap inspection by Health and Safety on all his building sites. I think I've spent too long being nice."

I tried not to remember the plant pot being lobbed through that window, and that it was a death which had sparked off all this. It was much better to treat it as a game.

"Where have all the llamas gone?" I asked Philippa in the kitchen that evening. "Are they in the maternity ward already?" I had missed their dimly calculating faces peering over the wall as I drove past on my way home.

Philippa scrubbed at the loam under her fingernails. "Some of them. The males and non-pregnant females are in that field next to the Hacienda for a few weeks, she's borrowed it from the farmer. I think the farmer hopes they'll escape, and rampage through the Eccles' garden." She paused, and hid her face in the sink, "I hear they're really partial to jam sandwiches. That's how they bribed them to walk into the trailer. Where are you going?"

I grabbed my jacket, "To the village shop before it closes. I need some fags."

Maggie found me at my table, trying to keep Curlydog away from the cheap sliced white loaf, the tub of dubious spread, and the pot of bright red jam.

"I'm going to have to ask," she said, pulling away from my sticky kiss, "what the fuck are you doing?"

"Making sandwiches."

She gave my hair a tug. "I can see that. We're not going on a picnic, are we?"

I put my arms back round her waist. I'd have to be careful, or I'd be waylaid from my plan.

"Don't be ridiculous, it's night, it's the middle of winter. I'm going to move some llamas."

"Jesus Christ." She sat down, and automatically shoved a piece of bread into her mouth, "Do I want to know this?"

I explained, and watched her shake her head, as if she was trying to wake herself up.

"I'm only giving the llamas a helping hand, and fulfilling the farmer's wishes," I said sweetly. "Look on it as a gift to the beleaguered agricultural sector."

"Give me strength. Haven't you had enough trouble with that vile man? You're. . ."

"Nuts," I finished for her. "I know. It's childish, it's vindictive, and you don't have to come with me."

She looked mournfully at the curtain. "And here I was, foolishly expecting Horlicks, a book at bedtime, and some hot sex. How wrong can a girl be?"

My knees wobbled. I kept myself from falling on her, and delving under her soft purple fleece.

"You can have all those," my voice was a mite squeaky, "when I've finished."

"You've no mercy. Give me a knife, then. I'll butter, and you can jam."

"Aren't we taking Curlydog?" Maggie's breath formed cloudy puffs in the air as we made for my car.

I opened the door for her, and bowed her inside. "No way. If she gets loose and starts barking, we'll be in real doo doo."

Maggie started wrapping a scarf around her head. "I'm going in disguise. Don't expect me to hang around if anyone sees us, I won't have any qualms about abandoning you and running away."

I threw the bag of sandwiches on to the back seat. "Just as long as I know where I stand. So I don't go into shock when my lover deserts me."

"You're lucky to have a lover at all. Drive, if we're doing this."

I parked on a verge well beyond the field next to the Hacienda, and we crept back along the lane. Maggie moaned about her footwear.

"These are my favourite shoes, they'll get ruined."

"Why didn't you say? I would have lent you my wellies."

"How silly of me not to ask. They're only six sizes too big."

"Do you want to go back to the car?"

"Do you want a thick ear?"

I kissed her by the gate into the field, tugging the scarf away from her mouth.

"I'm teaching you new skills," I said, replacing the folds. "You never know when this could come in handy."

She started climbing the gate. "Yeah, the next time I'm in the Andes. Where are they, anyway?"

I followed her over. The field sloped upwards, dark and soggy, the winter grass lumpy under my feet. I tried to flash my torch discreetly, and its beam caught a dirty white blur.

I pointed, "There. They're all huddled in that little hollow. They must be sleeping."

"Aren't they cold?"

"They're used to high altitudes, aren't they?"

She stopped abruptly. "Do they bite?"

I bit my lip. "I don't know. Maybe they spit, like camels."

"Maybe they kick, like mules. You should have read up on this."

I gripped the bag tighter. "We've got our secret weapon. Hang on, we have to make this easier for them."

At least I had guessed one thing right. The boundary between the field and the garden was neither a sturdy fence nor a thick hedge, but an old dry stone wall, bulging in places where over a century of tree roots expanding underground had shifted the earth. I did another torch sweep, and found my spot, a short stretch which had lost its neat capping stones. I advanced towards it.

"I hate to do this," I said over my shoulder, "but it's all in the interests of neighbourliness."

Together we worked to lower the wall, arranging the stones we removed to make it look like my idea of a natural collapse. As quiet as we tried to be, the grinding and clattering were horribly loud. I wiped my brow, and took my hundredth look at the silent expanse of the garden.

"Shit, that'll have to do. If they can't climb over that, they're a disgrace to their species."

Maggie let me walk in front of her, as we approached the dozing beasts. So far, they had shown no interest whatsoever in our activity. I pulled a sandwich from the bag, directed my torch beam on it, and spoke to the nearest animal.

"Here, lovely llama, look what we've got for you."

In the faint outer rim of torchlight, a pair of half-shut eyes blinked, and a supercilious lip curled.

"Perhaps it's the wrong kind of jam," Maggie said from a good few yards away.

I waved the sandwich closer. I had an imprecise notion of engaging the animals' attention, then laying a tidy trail to the tempting hole in the wall. Just in time, I yanked my hand back from a set of snapping yellow teeth. There was a collective stirring in the hollow, a creaking of knees, then I was flying across the field, hurling jam sandwiches over my shoulder. At the gap, I performed a desperate swerve, threw a last handful over our rockfall, and stood flat against knobbly stones as the press of determined smelly bodies barged through the wall and galloped off into the exciting manicured spaces of the garden. I stumbled to the gate. Maggie was already on the other side, holding on to the bars, her legs crossed.

"Oh God, help. . .I've never seen. . .the look on your face. . ." She surrendered to her laughter, a fish released into its natural element.

"Ssh, ssh," I put my hand over her scarf, "we mustn't blow it now."

We rocked down the lane, snorting breathy plumes and wheezing like a pair of ancient drunks. At the car, instead of bolting inside, Maggie leaned back against the driver's door, undid her scarf, and grabbed my hips. She had stopped laughing.

"You're having a very bad effect on me." The urgency in her voice was startling.

I bent my head, her mouth opened, and her hands moved.

Forked lightning shot through me.

I groaned. "It's a very good effect. Let's get home." Her hand moved again. "Christ."

It was too cold out here, the ground was too wet, a car might drive by... if she stopped now, I wouldn't be able to stand it. I fumbled for the door. "Can we..."

It was fierce and cramped and brief and unladylike, and so glorious that for a moment I thought the car had rolled over.

"I don't care if you think I'm kinky," Maggie's embarrassed face hiding was becoming familiar, "it's you in your boots. I find it such a turn on."

I made her smile. "Sweetheart, it's not kinky, it's a useful revelation."

She tried to sit up, "This is shameful. We're grown women. What if someone had walked by?"

I scrambled into the front and pulled up my jeans. "I wouldn't have noticed. I'm loathe to tell you this, but there's one more little thing I have to do."

I drew up outside the farmer's house, and jumped out of the car. I was relieved to see a light on in a downstairs window, I wouldn't have wanted to wake him up if he was an early to bed, early to rise merchant. I stopped at Maggie's tap on the driver's window, and turned back.

"What?" I mouthed at her grinning face.

She wound the window down. "You're walking funny," she hissed, then slid smartly back to her own seat.

I pulled an infantile face, and composed myself to knock at the door.

"Yes?" He was short and barrel-chested, with arms that could fell a frisky heifer.

I tried to be conscientously concerned. "Those llamas?" He nodded. "I was driving past. They're in Orchard House's garden. They must have got over the wall."

He said nothing for a moment. The news was starting up on his television. "Right you are. Is the gate on their drive shut?"

"Yes." This had been a vital element. I didn't want the poor animals wandering out on to the road.

"Right you are." His expression didn't change. "The morning'll do. No good chasing after those daft critturs in the dark. Cause more damage."

"That's true." I smiled, he smiled, and he scratched his bristly chin.

"Bring that funny little dog of yourn over for some ratting one day if you want. Sunday afternoons are always good for me."

"Thanks."

"No, thank you."

I left him to his television, and did a special bandy-legged walk back to the car for Maggie.

"Maggie," in bed that night I remembered something, "would you say I had a snotty expression?"

"You don't at the moment."

I kissed her fingertips, "No, I mean in general."

She pretended to think. "Not snotty, I wouldn't say. More, how can I put it, glacial."

"Glacial?" I should never have brought this up.

"Mm. It's part of your appeal. Makes women like me want to thaw you."

"I'd say you'd succeeded big time, darling." I hadn't quite planned the endearment.

"You're being very sweet. Is it because you've discovered my inner slut?"

"No, it's because I love you." That was so unplanned that I froze.

"Thank God for that. I thought it was just me."

"You mean. . . ?"

"I don't go rustling livestock and bonking in cars for any passing fancy. Of course I love you."

I went for broke, "Is this a relationship, then?"

"I should damn well hope so, llama girl. You didn't save any of those sandwiches, did you?"

Chapter 17

Naturally, it was pure chance that I had to drive past the Hacienda early the next morning on my way to deliver a chair for Frances. It was equally fortuitous that I was in her van, which was considerably higher up than my car, and that I had to slow down to a crawl near the house. You never knew when a tractor might appear around the next bend. Curlydog did a double-take, and put her front paws against the passenger door to get a better view. The llamas had gravitated to the house, and were nibbling speculatively at window boxes and potted shrubs, their faces lost in contented curiosity. As I watched, a shrieking figure, a golf club in her hand, came out of the front door. The animals shied away and scattered, adding more pock marks to the lawn, and the largest jumped up on the bonnet of the silver Mercedes in the drive, where he relieved himself copiously. I thought the better of offering our services to help round up the invaders, even though, with Curlydog's help, I could have increased the mayhem significantly, and had to pull into the hedge, when a car coming in the opposite direction in the middle of the road stopped blatantly in front of the Hacienda's gate. The three elderly ladies inside strained to see up the drive, their hands fluttering to their mouths, and their eyes round. One of them turned to smile at me, and waved delightedly, as if we were spectators at an unscheduled royal visit. Another car came to halt behind me, and the ladies helpfully pointed up the drive, guilty pleasure bobbing their neat perms. Smiling in my turn, I drove merrily on my way, thinking how pleasant it was to be part of the community.

"The best part of it," Philippa informed Maggie and me just before we left for the pub quiz that evening, "is that the boundary between the field and the garden is Orchard House's responsibility. That's what they were saying in the village shop anyway. The Eccles won't have a leg to stand on if they try litigation again."

"What a shame about their garden," Maggie said insincerely. "None of the llamas were hurt, were they?"

Philippa looked beadily at us, "Not that I've heard. Where were you two off to last night?"

"A quick visit to the pub," I breezed. "Come on, my love, while I've still got my trivia head on."

"I hope you know a lot about Sixties' TV programmes."

We made good our escape, before Philippa fingerprinted us, and demanded samples of our DNA.

The following Monday morning, I lay in a luxurious stupor, quite unlike my usual wary assessment of the week ahead. Maggie had the day off, and had gone to sleep again, her arm over me and her breathing dissolving into mine. We were going to spend her paycheck on clothes for her in Millford's finest emporiums, interspersed with vanilla slices at Benn's, and then proceed to her house, where we would no doubt amuse ourselves quite successfully before her pleasant housemates returned from work. In the interests of being even-handed, we had spent one night there, but although her friends had been welcoming and accepting, we had decided that the outhouse was more private. Besides, Curlydog had behaved very badly, demanding to be let out at three in the morning, and ram-raiding a cupboard when no-one was looking. I hadn't shared her innocent pleasure in trails of flour and sugar through the house. I peeked over the edge of the bed, and grinned at the one twitching paw poking out from under her blanket. I guessed she was re-living her afternoon's ratting, when she had delighted the farmer and herself with three sad corpses. In a minute, I would get up and make some coffee, and maybe some toast. . .

"Nice," Maggie muttered dozily at my hand moving across her back.

"Breakfast?"

"Angel." Her eyes remained determinedly shut, but her legs shifted.

Coffee or more canoodling, I thought, what a dilemma. The phone saved me from this stark choice.

"You're not still in bed," Heather spoke at twice her normal speed. "Come on, get in gear, get your suit on. Today's the day, you're my paralegal, and we're going to bugger up Eccles' Monday."

"But Maggie's here," I said stupidly, "we're going shopping."

"Wake up! You said you wanted in on this, we're not waiting till you've worked your way through the Lesbian Karma Sutra. It's now or never, Mrs Woman."

"Is there a Lesbian Karma Sutra?" Maggie was tickling the nobble at the top of my spine, and I was coming out in goose-bumps.

Heather squealed. "How should I fucking know? Are you coming, or shall I ask Vin to dress up and be in at the kill?"

"No!" At my raised voice, Curlydog started shuffling out of her box, making her 'Hm, I think I need a pee' face. Now I had three pulls on my attention. "Can Maggie come as well?" I ventured.

There was a conference at the other end of the phone.

"Why not." Heather sounded resigned. "But she'll have to look respectable, like another lawyer or my PA. Now stop farting around, and get your idle butt to the Big Top asap."

"Yessir. Toodle-oo." I clicked off the phone, and kissed Maggie's raised eyebrows. "I have to let the dog out. Fancy a change of plan?"

She was scrabbling about with her clothes before I had finished explaining.

"So you're keen?" I asked, watching her toss aside her jeans.

"I'm not letting you out of my sight. Quick, into the house shower, then we'll have to nip by my place for my interview outfit. I've always wanted to venture into the criminal underworld, and it's better than llamas."

Even though I broke several speed limits on the way to the Big Top, Heather was already on the pavement, flanked by three men wearing dark suits and stony, cauliflower-eared faces.

"What kept you?" she asked. "Wait for them to bring their car round before we set off. You're very smart, Maggie. Hurry up with that chair, Sarah, and don't squash my case."

"Who are they?" Maggie looked out of the back window at the black car drawing up behind us.

"Armed guard. Let's go, the sands of time are trickling through the hour-glass of retribution. Left at the lights. How's the raffia work going, Maggie?"

"Not as much fun as the lawyer business obviously. Where did you get that jacket? I'm looking for something similar in grey."

We were approaching Eccles Construction before I had time to butt into their exchange of fashion tips. I stopped well before the office building.

"What are we doing here?"

Heather gave an annoying smirk. "That's a very metaphysical question. Do you mean are we part of some divine plan for the universe, or merely a random product of billions of years of astrophysical events? You're asking the wrong person, pal. Don't stop here, it'll be a pain for you to push me so far."

I switched off the engine. "I'm not going in there, and I'm doubly not going in there until you tell me what's going on." The last three words sounded very loud without the motor running.

Heather pretended to be surprised. "What's your problem? We're only delivering some papers to Eccles about a loan. It's all above board. The chaps will take me in if you won't."

I looked in the rear-view mirror. The driver of our escort lifted a forefinger, and gave me what he probably thought was a reassuring smile. It was so alarming, that I restarted the engine, and placed us in front of the office door.

"Glacial or what," Maggie said in an undertone as I pushed Heather's chair. "Go with the flow, babe."

I snarled. "Doesn't it worry you that we're about to face Eccles in a state of complete ignorance about why we're here?"

She shrugged. "Just like the inter-departmental meetings I go to. I'll get the door."

The receptionist wasn't happy to see us. She showed us the whites of her eyes, dived behind the shelter of a desk, and picked up a phone. Heather tapped on the glass of the hatch, ignoring the hand shooing us away.

"Yew'll have to leave," the unfortunate woman wasn't risking opening the hatch, and her words were muffled, "I'll call security." She was breathing quickly, an uneven flush showed under her make-up, and her fingers trembled on the phone.

Heather gave the glass a shunt, and it slid open, producing an 'eek!' from the other side.

"I think you'll find Mr Eccles is expecting us. Check his diary. I'm here to represent McLaren Byron. And sign here, please." She pulled a manila envelope from her case, and extracted what looked like a receipt with at least two carbon copies. The receptionist stayed put, perhaps fearing that if she came closer, we would heave her through the hatch and disrupt her hair-sprayed coiffure.

Heather sighed. "All right. We'll go through the building until we can find someone who can write their name. He'll do." An oily-haired man in a cheap suit materialised, walking towards us from the end of the passage.

"Do you work here?" Heather was all sweet reason.

"I do. Ian Saunders, Sales. How can I help?" The mingled smell of stale sweat and aftershave, coupled with a dollop of salesman smarm, was not at all attractive.

"Could you sign here for receipt of these papers for Mr Eccles senior? We're having a hitch with the receptionist."

He gave the official-looking envelope only a cursory glance. "Sure thing, ladies." A click of his ballpoint pen, an ostentatious signature, and I saw a definite wave of relaxation sink Heather further back in her chair.

"Thank you so much. This copy's for you." She ripped off the flimsy paper, "Maybe if you could see that Mr Eccles gets this. . . ?"

His smile was as greasy as his hair, "Anything to oblige. Not good weather today, is it? The winters here go on for ever. I don't know about you, but it makes me want to jump on a plane and seek out some sunshine ha ha. Still, my fiancé and I are lucky, we have the next best thing, a heated conservatory, sit there on a Sunday morning with the papers, and we think ourselves on to that Greek island. How about you? I expect at least one of you has one, don't you?" He took our bemusement for denial. "Surely, they're so reasonable nowadays, when you think of how property values are shooting up. Here," he dug in his jacket pocket, and brought out a snapshot, "this is ours. We went for the art deco look, my fiancé's a bit of a design student, Charles Rennie Mackintosh, Arts and Crafts. . . Although you can get a range of different styles, if you're more into traditional Victoriana, or maybe modern minimalism. . ."

Maggie seemed far too interested in the photograph. "Nice plants. And I like that stained glass. I bet it makes for a lovely light in there."

She may have missed out on her shopping trip, but I wasn't going to let her leave here with a conservatory for a house she didn't own. "I think we've finished. . ."

"Saunders!" A harsh bark ended the sales pitch. "Get out of here, man. These people are time-wasters. I want you on the phone to those property companies now."

The salesman scuttled off, not before Heather had snatched back the envelope and receipt.

"Good. You've appeared. Now we can have our meeting." She spoke as if he wasn't advancing on us like the Assyrian coming down like the wolf on the fold.

"You're babbling, woman. Leave now, before I call the police."

"McLaren Byron, Monday am, that's us. Shall we use the conference room?"

He stopped a few feet away. I would have appreciated knowing who or what McLaren Byron was.

"Don't make me laugh. You're a washed up associate of criminals. And she's not a paralegal," he pointed at me, "she's a local headcase. I don't know who your other hanger-on is, but if she knows what's good for her, she'll leave you to push yourself home."

I had never admired Heather as much as I did then. Her words came out clear and precise.

"Your attitude is very strange, Mr Eccles, I'd much prefer to do this in private. Since you're being so obstructive, however, I'll proceed here. McLaren Byron have retained me to ensure you receive these documents. I have obtained the necessary receipt from one of your employees, and I am now handing them over to you." She held out the envelope. "I have also been instructed to answer any initial queries you may have about them. I would be grateful if you could read the covering letter now, so that I can fulfil this obligation."

"This is a joke." He grabbed the envelope, and ripped out its contents. As he scanned what I took to be the letter, a tic appeared in the corner of his right eye. The page crumpled in his fist.

"You can't fool me. You've made this up. I'm ringing them now, and you'll be in serious trouble. Don't you know who I am? The courts won't see this as a little practical joke." He was still riding the wave of his righteous anger, yet I detected a wobble in his board.

Heather indicated the receptionist's office. "Please do. I'll speak to Mr Byron himself. In fact," her phone was in her hand and she was pressing keys, "I'll get him on his mobile now. The landline to his office is always so busy. Ah Nick," she became apologetic, "is this a bad time? Slight bother at this end with Mr Eccles. Could you have a word with him, put his mind at rest that I'm working for you? Ta." She passed Eccles the phone. "There you go."

It must have been the combination of her patronising tone and whatever Nick, whoever he was, said. The phone crashed against the wall, and a foot was aiming at Heather's chair.

"You bitch. I'll fucking. . ."

"Now now, sir. That's not how we speak to ladies." A beefy hand spun Eccles round, and another beefy hand went to his sternum. It only looked like a little tap, but Eccles fell back against the wall.

"Heuuuw." He was clearly winded.

"No-one has any manners nowadays. I came in the back way. Shall we go?" Our rescuer straightened his dark jacket, and smiled his terrifying smile.

"Thanks, Mr Barker." Heather was checking her footplates.

"You're welcome, Ms Shaw. A very hot-tempered and rude gentleman I'd say. He didn't get you, did he?" He made to give Eccles another tap.

"No!" Heather lifted her hand, "We don't want to over-egg the omelette."

"Quite so. I'll see you to your car. I'd say Mr MacRanald will be very pleased with this morning's work."

He ushered us to the door, where his companions waited, one on either side of the entrance.

"Mr Griffiths, Mr Morris, would you help Ms Shaw with her chair?" He stood facing the way we had come, thoughtfully rubbing the fingers of his striking hand.

"Are you expecting Gnasher Bell?" I hoped I sounded politely informed, not frightened out of my wits.

"Not really. He's not a morning person. Still, you can't be too careful."

He stayed in position until we were in the car and I was revving up the engine, then moved without haste to his own vehicle.

"And who the hell is he?" Of all the questions I wanted to ask Heather, this popped out first.

"One of Vin's merry men. There's something delightfully old-fashioned about him, don't you think?"

"What, like rickets or TB? Heather, what do you think you're doing? He could have. . . it could have been a bloodbath, haven't you had enough violence? I'm worried about you. . ."

"Och, get off your high horse, Miss I've Never Kicked a Man in the Bollocks. It was me that nearly got my chair knocked over. I expected Eccles to get shirty, so would you be if you'd just been bankrupted. Red light!"

Luckily I hit the brake and not the accelerator.

"Bankrupted?" I had booted a stranger, I could probably whack a friend around the head until she spoke sense to me.

"That's what we did, my little chums. I have to let Ran tell you the story, it's his great achievement. He's giving us lunch again." She turned to Maggie, "You as well, of course. Did you really like that conservatory?"

After several attempts, Maggie found her voice. "I'm a sucker for sales patter. I was already choosing the plants I'd have. Maybe a vine. Green light, darling. I wonder if any of the big DIY chains are doing deals on conservatories at the moment."

I rolled across the intersection. "You're not having one."

"It's not up to you."

"You don't even have a house, you fool."

"And who says my landlord wouldn't let me put one up? It would add value to the house."

I took both hands off the wheel. "Aaagh! This is pointless. Not another word."

There was a minute's silence.

"Philippa might like one," Maggie was imitating Curlydog keeping hold of a stick. "How about you, Heather? Could you fit one on your house?"

From his discreet tailing position, three cars back, Mr Barker must have wondered how I had ever passed a driving test.

Chapter 18

"There she goes!" Ran pulled his hand away, and the champagne cork hit the ceiling. He filled the waiting flutes on his desk, "Sure I can't tempt you, Sarah?"

I spoke through another smoked salmon sandwich, "No, really, it'll make me feel terrible. I'm quite happy with this." I lifted my glass of mineral water.

He blinked through the fumes of a cigar stuck at a rakish angle in the corner of his mouth, and distributed the flutes. "My lovely lawyer, my lovely security manager, the lovely friend of my lawyer's lovely assistant, the... handsome and erudite Mr Whippy." I wondered if he had been hitting the malt before we arrived. "A toast. To the triumph of good, and the destruction of the evil Eccles empire. May the force be with us, heh heh."

We raised our drinks, and made suitable 'hear hear' noises. Having ceased to be surprised at anything, I had greeted Whippy with nonchalance, and introduced Maggie to him. He had bent his scruffy head, and kissed her hand.

"I sense you are a beautiful person, not a corporate slave. Do you want a microwave?"

I had dragged her away to meet Ran, before she committed herself to buying a whole range of dodgy electrical appliances.

"I thought it would be a nice gesture to ask Whippy along," Heather was being the hostess of a cocktail party, "he's always been such a help."

I looked at Vin eyeing him up with a mixture of bewilderment and interest, and wondered if he was rough enough around the edges for her.

Ran tapped his glass so that it sang. "Storytime. I need to fill some of you in with some details. Are you sitting comfortably?" He was so pleased with himself, that if he was pricked with a pin, he would whizz around the room like a released balloon.

"Wait a mo'," Maggie squeezed a final few olives on to her plate, then settled down next to me. "We're ready."

Ran exhaled, creating an effect not dissimilar to a smoke bomb going off in front of the enemy's trench. "Today is the culmination of nearly two years' work, and I admit, I couldn't have done this by myself. No, no," he waved a modest hand at our 'surely nots', "I have been lucky enough to have the unwavering support of McLaren Byron, which has been the key to my success."

"Who are they?" I asked, sensing that he was begging the question.

"Loan sharks," Heather whispered.

He had heard. "No they are not. They are a perfectly respectable finance company, providing loans for entrepreneurs whom the stuffy banks are far too unadventurous to back. They helped me."

"And Nick Byron is your cousin," Vin added.

"Once removed. Anyway, we go back a long way. They're based in London, naturally, but they have a great interest in regional regeneration, and are experts at bringing movers and shakers together to do deals to benefit areas suffering from post-industrial blight, without involving all the government red tape and pen-pushing bureaucracy which stifles enterprise and business creativity." He grinned like a boy, "And all that shite. So, about eighteen months ago, Eccles was invited by a Pedersen's executive to a discreet dinner in London, at which Nick Byron happened to be present. Eccles toddled along in his best bib and tucker, and nearly had an orgasm at what the Pedersen's man told him in strictest confidence."

"Which was?" Maggie was getting the hang of letting Ran shine.

"That Pedersen Engineering were going to consolidate their holdings in Britain by closing their remaining yard on Tyneside, and relocating their head office and administration from London to Millford. Which would mean," he wanted to make sure we had got the point, "as the executive explained, a lot more work for the yard in Millford, and a sizeable influx of well-paid managerial types, who would all want top of the range housing, and facilities hitherto sadly lacking in Millford, like cafe-bars and exclusive health clubs." He paused to swig champagne and attempt a smoke ring.

"Is this true about Pedersens?" I hadn't heard any rumours of such a momentous move.

Ran winked. "I doubt it. What would a Norwegian sailor in a suit know about them? He just repeated what Nick told him to say. Eccles was fooled, though. And with Nick Byron there to egg him on, he cooked up a foolproof business plan. He would buy up most of the Sink, convert the slummy old flats into desirable penthouses with saunas and God knows what, and make a killing when the move happened, and property prices in Millford finally rose above the Great Depression level. Being the greedy bastard that he is, he didn't want any partners to help with the investment and take a share of the profits, so he borrowed a whacking load of dosh off McLaren Byron, putting up his house and business as collateral." He twirled his glass, "How sad for him when Nick Byron discovered that Pedersens weren't moving lock, stock and barrel to Millford, and today demanded immediate repayment of the loan in accordance with the small print in the contract, which he had previously assured Eccles was merely a legal formality." He ran out of breath, and sat back, wreathed in smiles.

"But. . ." I tried to see some flaws in this.

Heather jumped in, "But nothing. The money Eccles borrowed is tied up in property which is worth less than he paid for it, and the banks won't bail him out. Unless a miracle happens for him, McLaren Byron will soon be the proud owners of a thriving construction business, a desirable residence in Byreby, and a chunk of old Millford."

Maggie frowned. "Wasn't it very risky for your loan shark friends? They must have gambled. . ."

"Squillions." Ran had recovered his wind. "They'll get it back in the long term, even if they have to go through the courts. The loan was perfectly legal, and Eccles would never be able to prove that McLaren Byron knew that the Pedersen's executive was a fake. No, my friends, I am a devious mastermind, and a man never to be crossed. Revenge is a dish best eaten cold, as we always said when the electricity was cut off. Another drink, anyone? Oh, one more duty I am compelled, much against my will, to perform." He picked up a phone.

"Who are you ringing now? The bailiffs to repossess his Mercedes?" I was realising that our llama stunt had been rank amateurism.

"I wish. No, my friendly reporter on the Gazette. I don't believe in cover-ups, even though some might say that this smacks of the business community washing its dirty linen in public. With any luck, Eccles' little set-back will be front page news."

He was right. It was on Wednesday afternoon that William came hotfoot back into the Art Project from the shop, and gave Heather and me the treat we'd been waiting for.

"Who'd have believed it," he said, brandishing the paper, "that Michael Eccles is in the proverbial."

We pored over the front page. "Local Businessman Could Be Bust," the inelegant headline yelled. Ran's reporter had, however, done a slightly better job in his article, which described how Michael Eccles, "the previously well-respected head of the Millford Development Agency and boss of Eccles Construction", was in massive debt to a "London-based finance company over ambitious plans to re-develop the part of Millford popularly known as 'the Sink'." Clearly well-briefed, the reporter twisted in the knife by adding that "calls were being made for an independent investigation into the MDA's purchase of Berkeley Dock," and hinting unsubtly that Eccles may have benefited financially from this deal. Unsurprisingly, in spite of the reporter's sterling efforts to track down Eccles for an interview, the errant mogul was unavailable for comment. We were invited to turn to the leader on page ten, which, in tune with the paper's populist, vaguely left-wing, ethos, fulminated against the naked greed and get rich quick attitude of our modern business culture, and how it jeopardised the honest working person's ambition to do a decent day's work for a decent day's wage, since who knew what would happen to the workers at Eccles Construction now?

Bridie was surprised at our salivating interest. "What's got into you two? I didn't know you were into the business news. Should I order you the Financial Times for your fag-breaks?"

I had a fourth satisfying look at the photograph of Eccles, probably taken from the archives and not very flattering. "No, we just don't like him. He lives in the village, and is really unpopular."

"And I thought the wicked flourished like the green bay tree," May contributed. "How nice to be proved wrong for once."

Heather was good at being hypocritical. "You have to feel a shred of sympathy for the poor man. There he is, one day a powerful fish in a small pond with everyone looking up to him, and the next exposed as a foolish gambler, and hounded by the press."

May was having none of it. "How are the mighty fallen. Serves him right, he sacked my nephew once. And I've heard his wife is a right cow. If there's any justice in the world, they'll both end up at the Jobcentre, being bullied by those mini-Hitlers to take jobs at MacDonalds. I'd go in every day for a Big Mac, just to laugh at them."

I imagined Eccles flipping burgers, and Evadne having to say "Enjoy your meal", and was seized by unholy joy. Although I doubted that justice would be so poetic, or that there was any sort of afterlife, I hoped that David's ghost would be giggling with us.

"All over bar the shouting," Heather said so that only I could hear. "It's back to Eamon Bannon for our excitement."

I picked up my cigarettes, "Thank goodness. What was it you said weeks ago about canvases? Shall we go outside and discuss it properly?"

We sat by the bins like old times, and I let myself feel that a defining period of crisis had ended, and that I might never have the relapse I had always dreaded.

"Shame on you, Curlydog," I groaned from under the quilt. "It's late, we're all meant to be asleep. Why can't you empty your bladder properly when I let you out last thing?"

She carried on whining and tapping the door.

Maggie let me go, "Oh dear, she could be jealous, and wanting to go and visit her labrador. Or maybe she's got kidney trouble."

"Damn, she hates going to the vets. She knows where I'm taking her, and leaps around the car like a Tasmanian devil. All right," I got out of bed, "I'm coming."

Bleary-eyed, I went to the door. At least it was Saturday tomorrow, and we could sleep in. "Out you go, if you must. Any more of this, and it's the V.E.T. for you. And no, you can't go up to the village to look for Ted. You're too old for discos and fooling around. . . I don't believe this, what is it now?"

She wasn't skipping off to her favourite spot, but was still whining, looking backwards and forwards between me and the barn end of the yard. I coughed. What on earth had Frances and Philippa put in that Rayburn? The smoke smelled terrible, more like a bonfire than decent logs and coal. Curlydog's whine changed to a growl, and her nose went forward.

"Is it a rat?" I tried.

A shape moved in the faint light from the restored bulb on the gable wall.

"Fucking big rat," Curlydog's face said, and she shot howling towards it.

"Christ." I grabbed my old coat. A burglar, I'd have to stop her getting kicked. Then it sunk into my foggy brain that the light was faint because it was obscured by thick swirls of. . .

"Smoke! Fire!" I screamed. "Maggie, call the Fire Brigade!"

One arm half in a sleeve, I hopped, skipped and jumped to the kitchen door. Hardly ever locked, it crashed open under my weight with a noise that would surely waken even Frances. I pounded hollering up the stairs to make sure.

"Fire, there's a fire in the barn, get up!"

Philippa's head came round their bedroom door.

"What?" She sniffed. The bonfire smell was everywhere. "Bugger."

"Maggie's calling the Fire Brigade," I turned and jumped back to the half-landing. "Get the cats, I have to find Curlydog." I tried not to picture the barn's inflammable contents; wood, sawdust, glues, resins, all Frances' stores and work in progress.

Maggie, wrapped in the quilt, was at the wash house door, holding out my boots.

"No time. Have you called them?"

She nodded. "I'll move the cars. Don't want them to blow up."

Her words faded from my ears as I skated towards Curlydog's barking, barely aware of the cold mud and stones hurting my feet. She had driven the shape against the wall of an old garage where Frances and Philippa kept their vans, and was dancing frantically around it, darting out of its reach and preventing its escape by a vicious display of teeth and snarls. As I came closer, the shape resolved into that of a podgy young man, a petrol can in one hand. With the arrival of reinforcements, Curlydog retreated growling to my side, the young man tried to make a break for it, and I stuck out my unshod foot.

"No you don't."

He went down with a thud that made up for the pain in my battered toes. With enormous presence of mind, I sat on him, and did up two buttons on the coat.

"Best girl, Curlydog. Come and bite him if he struggles."

He ignored my threat. "Get off of me."

He was heavier than me, but not very fit, and I easily shoved his face back to the ground, while Curlydog made for his ankles.

"Oow!" His scream was drowned by the whine of a car engine as Maggie reversed at speed past us. I heard her pull the car on to the verge, and come running back.

"Who's that? Shall I sit on him as well?" She sounded quite keen, and her practical voice drew the nightmarish sting from my panic.

"It's Eccles Junior, arsonist. I can manage. Maybe you should move my car next..."

Through the chaos, I couldn't help noticing that although eye-stinging smoke hung in swathes around us, there was none of the crackle and roar of Frances's entire livelihood going up in flames. I became aware of two semi-naked figures yelling furiously at each other and pulling a hose-pipe towards the barn door.

"I told you never to do that!"

"It might have saved your stuff, quick, soak the door first, then we'll open it."

I shouted out in vain, "You'll let all the oxygen in. Wait for the Fire Brigade."

"Not fucking likely. Maggie, get some rakes from the tool-store. Stand back, Philly." Frances opened the door, and directed the hose inside. There was no explosion or wall of flame, only the densest eruption of smoke and steam. Unwilling to move from my captive, I watched the three banshee shapes stagger in and out of the smog, pulling at black mounds, stamping, choking, and going back for more. Even yards away from the action, my eyes were streaming and my lungs labouring, and, half-remembering some emergency fire drill, I pushed Curlydog's face closer to the earth, where the air might be cleaner. At the moment when it looked like the banshees might be winning, the night breeze carried the wail of sirens to us, and my prisoner gave a mighty heave, leaving me on my back with my legs in the air. I fought to stand.

"Stop him, stop him."

He didn't stand a chance. Caught between Maggie's rake and Curlydog's tireless pursuit, he was felled again, and this time, Maggie did sit on him, landing with an inconsiderate thump.

"Hope you're not a fussy eater. They always send arsonists to prison. Or to secure mental hospitals where the serial killers hang out."

His mouth worked, "Please, let me go. It was a mistake, I'll pay..."

I limped over. I was relieved to see that Maggie had exchanged my quilt for a coat, although it was hardly less revealing.

"What with? You're bankrupt." I gave him false hope, "Tell me what happened to David Hall, and we might consider..."

His words fell over each other. "He tried to blackmail my father.

Said he wanted a donation for Monk's House, or he'd tell about the dock. My father sent Gnasher to pick him up for another talk, and he freaked, he ran into the mud, let me go now, they're coming..."

The blue lights danced along the hedgerow, and I had to shout above the sirens.

"Fuck you. Manslaughter and arson. Your dad can keep you company in jail, you worthless piece of shit."

The firemen leapt out of their engine, and found us, four grimy unsuitably-clad women and a knackered dog, surrounding our hysterical arsonist.

Chapter 19

Curlydog was the heroine of the hour, and accepted a stream of plaudits, petting and pieces of cake as if it was no more than her due. Even Doris and Ethel, trying to look dignified as they crept in from their refuge in the toolshed, forbore to hiss at her, and almost gave her kindly glances, and the firemen, clustering round in the kitchen, broke off from criticising us for putting out the fire ourselves.

"She's a bright little thing," the hunkiest said. "The number of people who are saved by their dogs, you wouldn't credit it. Although she's no substitute for smoke detectors. I can't believe you haven't installed them, in an old place like this with solid fuel stoves and open fires. And I don't like the look of that wiring in the workshop. I strongly recommend that you get it sorted, and put in a sprinkler system. It could have been very unpleasant, and you were reckless to say the least."

"Ah, but I knew it was the hedge clippings which were smouldering away, and that nothing else had caught." Philippa was unrepentant. In defiance of Frances' express instructions not to clutter up the workshop with junk, she had dumped a van-load of hedge clippings just inside the barn door, with the intention of removing them to our elaborate composting factory in the vegetable garden before Frances got up on Saturday morning. We had worked out that Eccles Junior's petrol soaked rags, which he had shoved under the ill-fitting barn door, had only succeeded in semi-igniting this unpromising material. He hadn't been invited into the house; he was in the fire-engine, guarded by two grim firemen, awaiting the arrival of the police. None of the fire-fighters, hardened by years of pulling people from deliberately started conflagrations, had much time for his incoherent story that he had seen the smoke, and had been on the verge of calling for help when he was attacked by a savage mongrel. Maggie had helped.

"You must have x-ray vision to have seen any smoke from the road. This place is far too well tucked away. It's not as if there were flames shooting up into the sky."

The leading fireman had been dismissive. "Phone yer solicitor, matey boy. He can meet you down the nick. Put him in the rig, and don't let him go."

We had been cagey, however, about his possible motives for setting us alight.

"He lives on the edge of the village, but we're not friends." Philippa feigned deep thought, and was as tranquil as a woman can be when she is wearing a quilted bodywarmer over a wincyette nightie and is covered in soot. "Perhaps he has a mental problem. Aren't a lot of arsonists seriously disturbed? Maybe he needs psychiatric treatment, not locking up."

The hunky fireman looked at her in disbelief. "He wants putting away where he can't get at any matches. He's bloody lucky your dog bit him, he could be facing a murder charge if the fire had got hold."

Eccles Junior didn't appear to be appreciating his luck when the police handcuffed him, and put him, none too gently, in the back of their van along with a couple of belligerent drunks. My grim satisfaction at this sight diminished through the long tedium of giving details and making statements, and reassuring the matter of fact police sergeant that we didn't need to go to the hospital to be checked out for smoke inhalation. I couldn't wait for the police van to leave, and for Frances and Philippa to give Curlydog one last hug before returning upstairs, freeing me to sit on the settee in the outhouse, with Curlydog on my lap.

"What is it?" Maggie asked cautiously.

I could tell that my face was grey and sweaty, and I felt sick. "I think she's wheezing. Oh God, what if her lungs have been damaged? I'll have to take her to the vet first thing. Or what if she falls asleep and stops breathing? There's an emergency number, I should ring it. Where's the phone book?"

Maggie gave me a funny look, and put her ear to Curlydog's flank. "If she's wheezing, which I can't tell, it's because she's full of cake. Don't worry."

"This was all my fault. I should never have started messing with Eccles. What if those clippings hadn't been there? Frances could have lost everything, the house could have burned to the ground, they might have died. I'm not a safe person to know, I bring nothing but trouble, maybe I really am bad. . . I'm not sane enough to be with you, it's not fair on you to be lumbered with me." My mind was racing down a dark shaft.

"Right." Maggie crouched on the floor in front of me. "Look at me." Her hands were calm on mine. "Stop now. Nothing terrible happened. You heard what the fireman said about the wiring, that barn's a towering inferno waiting to happen. I've seen Frances in there with a power saw, a radio, a heater and a kettle all in one plug, it's a miracle she hasn't blown it up already. This has done her a favour, she might sort it out now. You're not looking at me."

I made myself meet her eyes. "But. . ."

"I'm not having this. Your rational mind knows that it's rubbish that you're a bad person. Which part are you going to listen to, the sensible part or the depressed part?"

"How do you know it's rubbish? How do you know the depressed part isn't right?"

She gazed levelly at me. "Like my mind was right after Carole split up with me, and it was telling me I was so fat and ugly that no-one would ever love me again, and I might as well lie on the railway line and wait for the Manchester Airport express to turn me into mince?"

I gazed back at her. "You didn't. . . ?"

She smiled briefly, "Well, obviously not, since I'm still here. Not that I didn't think of it every day for a few months." She let go of my hands, and sat next to me. Curlydog relaxed on my chest, and shut her eyes. "Nobody's perfect. If you had cancer instead of depression, you wouldn't say you shouldn't be with me."

My pulse was slowing. "This is different. I can't live on my own like an adult any more. I probably need you to function so well, and that's not healthy. . ."

She gave an impatient wriggle, "Oh what crap. Who's to judge what's healthy and what isn't? Frances and Philippa need one another, they couldn't do half of what they do if they weren't together. I need you, I'm useless on my own. Before I met you, I wouldn't have got out of bed some days at the weekend if my housemates hadn't been there. I would have stayed under the covers with a bottle of sherry."

I was stymied. "Oh."

Her hand was playing with my hair. "I'm sorry, you're not the only person in the world who's screwed up. I could easily slip into being an alcoholic if I didn't watch myself."

Warmth from her thigh and Curlydog's hairy body eased the painful buffeting of my heart. "So, we're just two inadequates finding solace in each other?"

"That's about the sum of it. What does it matter if you need me to keep you sane, or I need you to stop me drinking too much? Heather needs Ran to perk her up, Ran needs Heather to look after. . ."

"What?"

She laughed at her cleverness. "It's clear as day. He loves having someone to care for. I picked that up right away."

I leaned into the comfort of her shoulder, "Ok, Mrs Freud. Shall we go back to bed for what's left of the night? Or do you want me to steal a bottle of Philippa's gin for you?"

"Yeah, and I'm driving you straight to Monk's House for an emergency admission." She unbuttoned her coat, "I wonder what the firemen made of the four of us?"

I carried Curlydog over to her box. "They're probably still gossiping about us. By the time the next shift comes in, we'll be a lesbian nudist colony with a penchant for dangerous wiring."

She fell into bed. "To aid us in our dubious sexual practices."

I decided to swallow-dive on top of her, "Don't give me ideas. Did you like their big boots?"

Her eyes widened, "Ra-ther. I say, I wonder if you could get hold of a pair?"

"I could try. But I'm not wearing them in bed, and wrecking my sheets."

"Who said anything about a bed? We could start another fire, get the engine out, and do it in the back of that."

We laughed ourselves to sleep, holding on to this relief from a damaged world.

The March sun was almost beaming down, birds twittered in hedges pregnant with buds, gangs of lambs skipped giddily in the fields, and I powered into a sprint finish, forging into the yard and collapsing on my doorstep next to Maggie.

"And Sarah Dunne crosses the line to win the World Cross-Country Championship!" she gabbled into a piece of firewood. "The title comes back to Britain! What a moment for this athlete, who has battled depression and doubt to smash the European record, and prove her critics wrong. Sarah," she held the piece of wood in front of me, "congratulations. Talk us through that incredible race. How does this make you feel?"

"Like shit. Get me some water."

"There you have it. The words of a champion." She lobbed the wood back on the pile in the yard, "You're really purple."

I stopped coughing. "I'm really buggered. I'm going to have to train more seriously if I'm going to do that half-marathon. Blimey." My lungs erupted again.

"That's a good healthy sound." She went inside, and came back with a glass of water. "You've got a couple of months. How far was that?"

"Only about eight miles." I gulped some water, and sweat jumped out on my forearms.

"It was quicker, though. Under seventy minutes. I timed you, sort of."

I wiped my wet forehead. Why had I let her persuade me to enter the Lakes May Dash? I would only show myself up, crawling over the line hours behind the leaders, along with the fun runners. It would be so humiliating to be beaten by a giant chicken, or a group of men carrying a Viking longboat. The glass of water was followed by a mug of tea.

"Don't say a word," I said, five minutes later, when I lit up.

"They're your lungs. Have you rung your agent?"

I lifted my tracksuit top and sniffed. "I must have a shower."

She put her hand on my back, "Don't change the subject."

I scratched my head, and caught the amusement in her eyes.

"Do you honestly think I should? Are they good enough?" Ages ago, I had let her see my animal cartoons, and she had been nagging me ever after.

"Darling, if we have this conversation once more, I'm going to ring her myself. They're brilliant. Let Frances and Philippa see them, if you don't believe me."

I smiled, and leaned back against the door. "I'll ring her soon. Where's the dog?"

She jerked her head. "Still digging her hole behind the toolstore. Can't you hear her?"

I concentrated, and heard the scraping and snuffling of a dog engaged on a serious mission humans wouldn't understand. On the toolstore roof, Doris and Ethel lay with their heads over the far edge so that they could monitor her progress. Since the fire, relations between the three had been markedly more amiable, and I wondered if they had some weird tunnelling project underway. Perhaps they were aiming to come up inside the kitchen cupboards. I smiled again, and took another drag without exploding. Maybe I would ring my agent very soon. I would need something else to work on after the mural had ended, something which stretched me more than drawing Easter bunnies at the Art Project. I turned so that I could see Maggie's face, her eyes shut in the sun and a smattering of earth from the vegetable garden on her cheek, and dared to think ahead. She was shelling out a lot of money in rent for a place in which she hardly spent any time, and my easy tenants in Eastgate had hinted recently that they wanted first refusal if I ever put the house up for sale. Would it be too soon to broach the subject of finding somewhere to live together? Village rumour had it that a rundown cottage with a large overgrown garden would come on to the market by the summer, and houses sold very quickly in Byreby. The Hacienda had been snatched up within a fortnight. My stiffening muscles twitched. Although Michael Senior and Evadne had disappeared from view, Michael Junior's case hadn't come to court yet, and I wasn't looking forward to our summons to appear as witnesses for the prosecution. The legal system had come down harshly on him, refusing him bail, so he was currently languishing on remand in an overcrowded prison, and I dreaded what secrets his defence would reveal. I elbowed this uncomfortable thought aside, and focussed on the present. Nothing bad was happening to me now, I'd had a good run, and could relax in the sun with my woman and a very smart car coming into sight. . .

Maggie opened her eyes. "Oh Lord, it's Bonnie and Clyde."

I used the doorframe to pull myself to my feet. Ran was looking frustrated, and Heather was waving a letter at me through the windscreen.

I felt chilly. "I hope that's not to do with the court case. We'd better bring a couple of chairs out if they want to sit in the sun."

Ran sprang out of the car, "Can you help me carry Heather to a seat? She's got some news for you. She won't tell me what it is."

She wouldn't tell me anything either until she was settled, and we had made more tea, then she gave me the letter.

"Read this." She was biting her lip.

I unfolded the stiff cream sheet. It was headed by a single word, "whiteroom", in lower-case designer typescript. "Dear Ms Shaw," I read with mounting horror, "we do not usually accept unsolicited material, but we have pleasure in informing you, as Eamon Bannon's agent, that we were very impressed with the samples of your client's work. Please ring Gregor Markovsky on the number below, so that we can talk about setting up a meeting with your client to see more of his art, with the view to exhibiting him in the near future. Yours in anticipation." The signature was an illegible scribble.

"Fuck," I whispered, "what have you done?"

Heather was laughing so much, Ran had to keep her upright.

"I sent off some photographs, including that canvas you did the other week, isn't it great?"

Maggie took the letter from my nerveless fingers, and clutched her brow. Eamon Bannon was another secret I hadn't been able to keep from her.

I forgot my athletic career, and lit another cigarette. "We'll have to stop this. We won't be able to carry it off, you've made your point. . ."

Heather's better leg moved, "Och, it seems such a shame. A trip to London would be just what the doctor ordered. I like being Eamon Bannon's agent."

It hit me that I was an impressive artist. Was there any way we could take this further? I would love Heather to have her fun in

London with these self-important gallery types. I went for the cruel reality.

"But he's not real. You can't set up a meeting and not produce him. He'll have to appear sooner or later, and then we'll be found out. I'm sorry, but I'm not turning into a drag king for you."

"Hm, why not?" Maggie murmured seditiously.

Ran's patience ran out. "What are you saying? Who's Eamon Bannon?" *Heather must be far better than me at compartmentalising her life.*

We both looked at him. A man in early middle age, unthreatening on the outside, clever, worldly-wise and without scruples on the inside. The same thought came to us simultaneously, and I saw it in Heather's analytical gaze. His clothes were too straight, his septum was intact, it might be impossible to persuade him to shave off the rest of his hair, dress down and speak in a Fife accent, and to teach him the content of an Arts degree in days.

I gave him a polite smile. "Ran, what do you know about art?"

Onlywomen Press Ltd. is a feminist lesbian publishing house.

Our titles, literary and popular fiction as well as poetry and non-fiction theory, are available from bookshops or libraries throughout the UK, Europe, Australia, Canada and the USA.

See our website, www.onlywomenpress.com, for more information.

Write for a free Onlywomen Press catalogue.

Mail Order Department
Onlywomen Press
40 St. Lawrence Terrace
London W10 5ST
England